The Dogs that Follow their Detective Dreams # 3: Syleria Susae and Vanessa Pana's Unicorn Mystery

By

I0543530

Sarah Cantu

First Edition, 2007

Dedication

This story is dedicated to all my friends and companions at Kingsway Christian School! It has been a wonderful school year with so much happening everyday and this story was inspired by each and every one of you!

Special thanks to my publisher, editor and Dad, Ricardo Cantu, my encouraging mom, Veronica Cantu who enjoys all my stories and the music I compose! I hope to keep on writing, keep on composing, keep on singing, keep on playing music, and keep on doing everything that helps to improve my talent!

Contents

Chapter 1: Puppy War

It seemed like an extremely boring day. Not only did it seem hot outside, but it was almost like the county was melting. Vanessa Pana and I had gone to the store with Mrs. Louis so we could purchase some more dog food. It's A LOT of work trying to feed eight dogs three times a day, seven days a week, four weeks per month, twelve months a year, for the next eighteen years. That's as long as a dog can live.

On our way out of the store, we stopped by a nearby booth that was selling lemonade, ice cream, delicious ice cube shaped popsicles. There weren't that many customers since all that desert seemed to be melting too.

If you're confused about who's telling the story, it's me, Syleria Susae! Today was August 4th of 2006! But you probably want to know about me, so I'll explain in further detail. I'm a four month old Dalmatian who has not developed her spots. I used to be an orphan, but am now adopted by two really nice people, Mr.

Maxwell and Mrs. Lydia Louis. We live in San Francisco, California in an apartment.

Our next door neighbors are Daniel and Kimberley McMartin. Their origins are from Scotland, Swedish, French, and a little bit of German. I'm not the only dog in the family, but have seven other canine friends. Pierre, Vanessa Pana, and Mario Marco live with me and my owners. My other four friends, Royal Romeo, Allie Angie, Delilah Mara, and Gabriel Gordon were adopted by the McMartins. We usually see each other a few times every week! We eight buddies run a club, "The Dream Detectives Dog Club!" I have a lucky role of being the president of our group. Here's some information on my friends:

Mario Marco is a brown standard poodle whose age is the same as mine. We both seem to have the same interests of reading books! Mario is the club's vice president. Whenever I'm not around, he takes over my job.

Pierre is a five month old Dalmatian whose owner died about two months ago. Before adoption, he lived at an old, dangerous garbage dump. I think he's extremely optimistic, bold, and brave. Usually a game he loves to play in order to pass the time is "Pirates."

Vanessa Pana is a seven month old pink standard poodle. Her natural fur color is actually white, but her previous owners dyed it pink and we intend to keep it that way. She was once at a shelter and almost euthenized, but was rescued by us! The fact is, Vanessa Pana is the eldest canine of the group. She is extra talented in art and her personality is taken as sweet, gentle, kind, and wise. Like her gentleness, her preference is to take life easy one step at a time.

Gabriel Gordon is a black five month old toy poodle. Not long ago, he was helped to escape a local city dog pound. But here's the thing, he loves EDUCATION! I bet that dog would sacrifice all his dog treats for pencils, paper, and who knows what else! His ultimate passion is learning science, chemistry, physics, astronomy, etc. For his upcoming birthday wish, he wants to eventually establish a physics school and a pharmacy for dogs! Either it's his brain or he's gone nuts! Almost every day he reads a couple of chapters from this chemistry book which is more than a thousand pages long. It's probably the thickest book in the world! The words are so tiny; you need to use a microscope! No wonder the author died right after the book was published! I wonder if Gabriel Gordon will die right after reading that book; which makes me wonder if he'll ever finish the whole thing!

Royal Romeo is the youngest of us all. He is three months old and his past occupation was being a working dog at a fancy hotel. One thankful reason why we have Royal is that he's our entertainer. He is hilariously funny and one of his past times is reading joke books like Calvin and Hobbes or Garfield!

Allie Angie is a six month old Dalmatian who enjoys writing stories, listening to music, and playing sports!

Delilah Mara is a four month old silver minature poodle. I hate to say this, but she can be quite bothersome sometimes. She's always curious about EVERYTHING! Once she babbled on and on, on how Mario Marco could not spell words correctly. I know this is true, since Mario Marco just isn't meant for writing and learning like Gabriel Gordon. But to us, Delilah Mara is somewhat like a critic. She writes all her thoughts down on a secret notebook. Well, it's not so secret because she carries it around almost everywhere and Mario Marco sometimes tells us what she writes without her knowing. I guess we have a "Harriet the Spy" in our family. Oh well, might as well get used to it. Our club has a notebook (not the secret notebook), where we write about the day's adventure.

Everyone except Delilah Mara writes positive comments. Lately, Delilah Mara has been rating us on how good we are at being HER friend and being a detective:

        Delilah Mara --- A+
        Vanessa Pana --- A-
        Allie Angie --- B-

```
Syleria Susae --- B+
Mario Marco --- F
Royal Romeo --- C+
Gabriel Gordon --- D
```

I told you that Delilah Mara was like a critic. You can never ever seem to score perfect without Delilah Mara always getting the A+. Mario Marco and Delilah Mara hardly get along with each other. Ever since our last mystery, they just don't seem to agree with each other's ideas. In our last mystery, they fought over who was right and who was wrong. Boy, what grouches! What does it take to get some peace and prosperity in the household?

Later we reached home and were greeted by our friends. Delilah Mara and Mario Marco offered to put away the groceries. The rest of us went into the loft to eat an afternoon snack and watch a little bit of TV. Everyone was comfortable and happy on the couches, chairs, and pillows, when we started to hear some loud shatters and heavy thuds from the kitchen.

Now let me tell you this. Mr. Louis was at work while Mrs. Louis was at home. "Would you check to see what Delilah and Mario are doing? Maybe you could give them a hand with the groceries," she suggested. Lately she had been doing A LOT of housework and I knew it was about time to help out. If you didn't know, Mrs. Louis is twenty two years old and Mr. Louis is twenty five. I know, they seem really young, but they are extremely great step parents! Mrs. Louis has brown hair and Mr. Louis has black. Ok, back to the subject.

I was on my way to the kitchen. As I opened the door, I ducked as an egg flew past my head and splattered on the stove. In front of me was a horrifying sight! Delilah Mara was on one side of the kitchen and Mario Marco was on the other. What really shocked me was that they were having a food fight with . . . our new store-brought GROCERIES! I guess they never seemed to notice me because they kept right on throwing things at each other. From old spoiled bananas to a freshly wrapped apple pie I would have gladly eat if it wasn't all over the floor, I watched the fight for quite a while.

The two rivals eventually destroyed our new groceries and started grabbing random things to throw at each other like dishes, pots, pans, and food from the refrigerator, the pantry, and kitchen cabinets. The walls were covered in food and the floor was completely filthy. Finally I just couldn't take it any longer! "STOP!" I exploded. The fighting instantly stopped and I angrily asked, "What do you think you guys are doing? You're supposed to be putting away the groceries, not destroying them and trashing everything else too! It looks like a tornado went straight through our kitchen! Can't you realize that Mrs. Louis has spent almost TWO HUNDRED dollars on all this food?!?" "But Delilah Mara didn't put the eggs in the refrigerator!" yelled Mario Marco. "Eggs are supposed to go in the pantry!" argued Delilah Mara. "The cereal is supposed to go in the refrigerator!" she continued. "No it isn't!" screamed Mario Marco. I could feel the ground shaking and fumes rising out of their tomato colored faces. In an instant, Mrs. Louis burst into the kitchen shouting, "What's going on?!?"

At that point, some nearby china plates cracked and crumbled away at the noise. Whoa, I guess we really were more than loud. Those plates were the last of the surviving dishes and now they were piles of little glass crumbs.

To tell you a fact, Mrs. Louis never ever seemed to rest from her household duties and now we know why. In the end, Mrs. Louis paddled Delilah and Mario and made them clean up the whole kitchen (which took hours), and sent them straight to their room where they would be grounded for a whole month. They were not even allowed to take a single step out of the apartment.

Instead of going out to play, their punishment was writing a five hundred word essay on what happened, how it happened, and why. When Mr. Louis arrived home, he was displeased with Delilah and Mario.

"You should be ashamed of yourselves for causing all this

monstrous destruction! Why can't you work together once in a while?" he shouted furiously. Then that argument started all over again. "But the eggs are supposed to go in the pantry along with the popsicles!" Delilah Mara yelled. "It does NOT!" argued Mario Marco. "You were arguing over THAT? What kind of worthless puppies are you?!? Silence and go to your room right now and write an apology letter to Mrs. Louis!" roared Mr. Louis who just had about ENOUGH of all this.

Delilah Mara and Mario Marco stormed to their bedroom with everyone's eyes watching them both to make sure they really did what they were told. "That should teach them a lesson," I thought.

I hate to admit it, but our day just didn't seem to go so well. At suppertime, I checked the mail to find a few magazines. Our owners probably forgot to check earlier, but because of the food fight, that kind of took our minds off of the mailbox. Wow, I never knew that two puppies could take your time away so easily.

Chapter 2: The National Geographic Magazine

I brought the magazines from the mail and set them on the table. The ones I found interesting were "Ranger Rick" and "National Geographic", my favorite magazines. Last week, I had signed up for a "National Geographic Readers Offer" where I pay $5.00 for a set of thirty National Geographic magazines. Once a week I receive one of the thirty I ordered and will get the next twenty nine delivered in the next twenty nine weeks!

I hopped onto a rocking chair and started to skim through the articles on every page earnestly looking for something interesting. A magazine can have up to fifty pages or more which is A LOT of articles about animals! Well, at least this was a way to pass the time and forget the incident in the kitchen. I found everything a little boring. Just facts about birds and safety tips on bumble bees was all, but not much. I sighed and yawned as Vanessa Pana joined me and sat on a nearby couch to read a monthly Ranger Rick magazine.

"Anything interesting?" asked Vanessa. "Not really. It makes me wonder why I spent five dollars of my allowance on something I didn't really want," I groaned. "Let me see your magazine, Syleria. There has to be something that catches your mind," she suggested as she picked up my magazine. "Have you even looked through the table of contents?" she asked. "No," I said flatly. The truth was, I didn't really care. I sighed and watched as she looked through each page saying stuff like, "Hmm that looks interesting . . . Yeah, right! As if the tooth fairy even existed! . . . Whoa, look at the size of that chicken's eye . . . Oh my goodness!"

I sprang from my seat and quickly asked, "What?!?" "It looks like the Los Angeles Scientific Society has found a unicorn in the San Francisco Zoo!" she replied. "No way! Unicorns? They're practically a myth! They're fake, unintelligent, silly, and too girly like the toy unicorns I saw with the new Barbie doll set that just came out this year! The unicorns are way too fat and ugly, anyway!" I argued. "But that's for the collection of Barbie dolls! We're talking about REAL unicorns, Susae. I f you don't believe me, why don't you come and take a look at this magazine page yourself?" she snapped. That's exactly what I did. What surprised me was that Vanessa Pana was indeed correct! There in the page of my magazine was a REAL, LIVE UNICORN! It was pure white with purple and strawberry colored streams of mane and tail. The unicorn was absolutely beautiful! It looked like an ordinary horse, but on its head was a long, pointy, gold horn with a little pink star on top that sparkled! I read the article about the unicorn:

Is it Magic or Myth?

A myth has come to life as a mysterious unicorn appeared in Germany in the continent of Europe a week and a half ago. This stunning creature was found by a banker named Robert Portman, a member of the Los Angeles Scientific Society. The unicorn is currently held in the San

Francisco Zoo. Go see the living myth of wonder and decide for yourself if this unicorn is real.

Vanessa Pana and I spent the rest of the day looking at the unicorn over and over again. We searched on the internet and viewed the zoo's website and sure enough, more of the unicorn's information was being displayed. The unicorn was a three year old female named Juniper Jade. And she was going to be on display and tickets to see her show were FORTY dollars each! As we looked at photo shoots of Juniper Jade, I noticed Delilah Mara coming toward us. She had come from her room to get a quick snack. She seemed to be curious at what we were doing. "What's up?" she asked in her sassy voice. "The Los Angeles Scientific Society has found their first live myth, a unicorn!" I announced. "Yeah right, as if I'm going to believe you guys! The internet can lie, you know," she remarked. "Well come and see for yourself," said Vanessa Pana pointing at the computer screen. "Ha! That looks SO fake! The horse looks like it went through a mega car wash or underwent plastic surgery or something! The mane looks like confetti and party streamers, plus her horn is probably an ice cream cone along with white paint to color Juniper's body. I wouldn't fall for anything like THAT!" Delilah retorted. "Why don't you read the zoo's bulletin board? The unicorn will be displayed in front of people and tickets seem expensive since everyone wants to go see the show," I explained. "Does Jade just stand there? I mean, what can she do?" asked Delilah Mara intently. "It says she can do circus tricks and tickets are FORTY dollars each!" added Vanessa Pana. "FORTY dollars?!? I'm definitely NOT wasting my allowance on staring at a horse with a glued on horn! I just can't believe you're wasting away your time on something as ridiculous as this!" complained Delilah as she walked away laughing, "Imagine a unicorn being real! That's the most unpredictable thing that could even happen!" Vanessa and I were REALLY mad at her. Well, she'll see! Even if nobody else except Vanessa Pana and I will believe in the unicorn, we will stay faithful to our theories.

That night while Delilah Mara was asleep in bed, I quietly tiptoed to her dresser drawer and pulled out her secret notebook. For some reason, I had a feeling she had written more. I could feel the ink heavily engraved on the pages. That is if ink has any weight at all. With a flashlight in hand, or should I say paw, I read what she wrote:

Vanessa Pana's nose looks a little red. Either she's been stung by a bee or she's turning into Rudolph the Red Nosed Reindeer. What would Santa Claus say on Christmas Eve? Would he actually replace Rudolph for Vanessa? I sure don't want a deer in the family. Here's a song I revised:

Vanessa the Red Nosed Reindog, had a red fiery nose,
And if you ever saw it, it would burn out all the snow,
Al of the other reindeer, threw snowballs at her all day,
They never let poor Vanessa take the lead in Santa's sleigh.

Then one foggy Christmas Eve,
Santa came to say,
"Vanessa with your nose so red,
why don't I put you at the back of
my sled?"
Then how the reindog gave in; her
nose blew up a chimney,
Vanessa the Red Nosed Reindog, you
go down in misery.

I clapped that notebook shut
and purposely misplaced it and put
it in Mario Marco's dresser drawer
instead of Delilah's. Sometimes I
just can't help it. If Delilah
won't let others believe in the
unicorn and have a fair chance,
then why should she believe in
Santa? I once stayed up all night
at Christmas Eve and I never saw
any Santa. I lit up the fireplace
anyway and the next morning, I
told Delilah Santa never came. She
saw the fire burning and she said,
"You almost burned Santa! No
wonder he skipped this house, you
moron! You could have hurt him!" I
pointed to the presents under the
Christmas tree. Delilah was
relieved but when she saw the
plate that still had milk and
cookies she cried, "You ruined
everything, Susae! Santa's
probably toast right and I bet he

burned up right before he could
eat the snack I worked so hard to
make for him!"

Chapter 3: The News Goes Around

It was August 5th and the time was about 3:35 p.m. I decided to check my email, which seemed a little full. I had gotten a letter from my favorite member of the famous detective team, the Feline & K9 Companions. Her name was Patience, an intelligent Siamese cat who was a few months older than me. We've been communicating for a couple of days now and so far, we have been really great friends!

Dear Syleria Susae,

We hope to have a new mystery to solve. Any news lately? Meow, Patience

I decided to email Patience about the unicorn in the zoo. That could also be something for them to look forward to.

Dear Patience,

You can't believe what I saw in a National Geographic Magazine! Our zoo has a real, live, unicorn! Maybe we could go together! Well, I've gotta go! Purr, Syleria Susae

Dear Syleria Susae,

That is a marvelous idea! I could ask my owner, Sophie. I can't wait to see the unicorn for myself! Meow, Patience

Well, at least I got that settled! I'll go call Patience and see how she's doing! I skipped to the kitchen to find her phone number, which is in Mrs. Louis's pocket book. I copied the number: 417-3890 and I waited until someone picked up the phone. Luckily, it turned out to be Patience herself! What a wonderful surprise!

"Hello! It's the LeLaine Residence, home of the Feline & K9 Companions. How may I help you?"
"It's me, Syleria Susae! How've you been?"
"Pretty good! Also, I got your email and I just remembered that I ordered this week's issue of National Geographic and I was able to find the article about the unicorn! My owner Sophie has to write an article for the Weekly Junior News! But for the subject of her article, she wants to write about the unicorn!"

"Wow, that's so cool! When does the article have to be sent to the newspaper company?"
"At the end of next week; Probably around Friday."
 "Did you want to come over to my apartment or did you want me to come over to your house?"
"You can come over. I'm not really doing anything today."
"Ok! Cool Idea! I'll be right over in about an hour or so."
"Well, I'll see you later!"
"Bye, Patience!'

　　　Now that it was settled, I could talk this out with Mrs. Louis. Hopefully, she'll agree to the idea. I went in the living room to find Mrs. Louis sewing one of Mr. Louis's shirts. She had a day off of work today and sewing is one of her favorite things to do. Vanessa Pana, Royal Romeo, Pierre, Gabriel Gordon, and Allie Angie were in the kitchen making some lamb chop sandwiches and beef n' chicken salads. I know, you're probably wondering how dogs could eat salads or even cook! We've had lots of cooking experience and we love our salads as long as they have meat in them.

"Mrs. Louis, could I talk to you about something?" I asked. "Sure," she replied as she set aside her sewing materials. I quickly explained the whole story about how Vanessa Pana and I found out about a unicorn in the county zoo and how Patience wanted to go see the unicorn.

In the end, Mrs. Louis agreed saying, "If tickets are forty dollars each, we could try to save some money. Your allowance has around thirty dollars and Vanessa Pana's has about fifthteen dollars. Maybe we could go next week. Why don't you go and discuss this with Patience? I could drive you over to her house for a while." I couldn't believe my ears! "That'd be awesome!" I cheered.

"What's so awesome?" asked Vanessa Pana who probably overheard our conversation. Mrs. Louis told Vanessa Pana about saving money that could be a way to buy zoo admission tickets. "Sounds cool to me!" exclaimed Vanessa Pana excitedly. "What sounds cool?" asked Pierre, Royal Romeo, Allie Angie, and Gabriel

Gordon who just stepped in the living room and had heard Vanessa Pana's excitement.

So it took another five minutes for Mrs. Louis to explain about the unicorn and what Vanessa, Patience, and I planned to do. It seemed like no one cared a bit about what Mrs. Louis had just said. "Oh, it's just another fake fun attraction," sighed Gabriel Gordon. "Wow, I wonder how they glue the horn on the unicorn's head," wondered Allie Angie. "And dye the mane and tail to look like something out of a birthday party. She practically looks like a living toy! Something around her just doesn't seem completely real," added Pierre. "How come everyone insists that Juniper's a regular horse who underwent a mad scientist transformation along with plastic surgery and a face lift?!? Does she really look THAT fake?!?" asked Vanessa Pana angrily. "The thing is, she IS a regular horse and she probably went through a mega carwash like Delilah Mara told us earlier today," Allie Angie concluded.

Later, Mrs. Louis did drive Vanessa Pana and I to Patience's house. We discussed our matter with Patience's owner's mom, Victoria LeLaine. Victoria LeLaine also seemed to agree, but she'd ask about the idea with her husband, Ricky LeLaine. "It seems very possible. Ricky and I always have extra money and we have more than enough. I'm sure we could take these three explorers for a little visit to the zoo. They've hardly ever opened up their fantasy world," she said. "And it could help Sophie think of what to write for her article she has to send to the Weekly Junior News. I think she could go too," added Patience. If you didn't know, we're capable of talking to our owners.

Also, the Weekly Junior News is a kids magazine. You can sign up and even become a member or get a job like writing articles and constructing ads for products. Sophie was a news reporter as you can see. "That would be an excellent idea!' exclaimed Mrs. Louis. As the two adults chatted away, Patience led Vanessa Pana and I to Sophie's room. Their house isn't what I'd call a mansion, but maybe something similar.

Lately, the Feline & K9 Companions have been taking a break from mystery solving and they don't plan to search for a crime to solve until later. As Patience led me up the stairs the second floor, I heard an extremely loud music coming from someone's bedroom. "Don't worry, it's just Hunter listening to more music. He likes heavy metal and that's what he's been obsessed with it lately. He listens to it like almost twenty four hours a day," reassured Patience. I was relieved to pass the loud room which was shaking so much that it looked like the door was about to fall right over and the walls were about to crumble. In a few seconds, I was in Sophie's room where she sat at a corner of her room on a chair in front of a table with a computer. From where I was standing, it looked like she was on the program of Microsoft Word. So far she had a title for her article, but nothing else. With a blank expression, she stared at the screen without blinking. Patience called her name several times before she FINALLY got our attention.

"What's up?" asked Patience. "Not much. But if you really want to know, this all just seems to be totally pointless! How can I write my article without any information or ideas? I don't think my title is interesting." Sophie moaned. I could tell she was in great distress. "Sometimes I wonder why I signed up for this job in the first place! I'm not much of a good writer and in school, I have a B in language arts," she complained.

"I think your article will have a pick up in no time, Sophie. There's no need to worry."

"I wish I could believe you, Patience."

"Here's the reason why we came here. Vanessa Pana, Patience, and I are on a mission to see if that unicorn is real. Your mom thought a trip to the San Francisco Zoo could amuse us on our adventure and give you pointers on your article," I spoke up.

"Really? That does really help A LOT!"

"Yeah! By the way, it could answer all our questions about that mystery unicorn!"

After we finished talking, Vanessa Pana asked, "What's the title of your article?"

Again that blank look appeared on Sophie's face. Vanessa Pana and I hopped onto the table and so far the title was, "Juniper Jade: The Living Unicorn." Now if you asked me, that sort of seemed a little unintelligent. "I think you need something a little bit 'eye catching.' You know, a title that people can't take their eyes off of and have to keep reading," I explained. "Now you tell me!" Sophie groaned. We went downstairs and our matter was settled. At trip to the zoo! To the fantasy world, here we come!

Chapter 4: Real or Fake? That's the Question

Part II: Delilah Mara

I can't believe I have to stay in my room for the rest of the month. Why can't I have my OWN bedroom? Not only I am cooped up in my home prison, but I am stuck with Mario Marco, my worst enemy! I think Syleria Susae and Vanessa Pana are just wasting their time on all this myth and fantasy stuff. How could they believe such things? Everyone knows unicorns are fake. Well, almost everyone. I hate being in my room! I despise this world! I have to get out of this situation, but how? That's it, I've had ENOUGH of this detention! I'll get the telephone and chat with Sheryl Star. I hopped off my bed and went in my room. At least Mrs. Louis wasn't home. I was just about to step in the kitchen when I felt a tough pull on my tail. I landed flat on my bottom and behind me was Mario Marco!

"What are you doing? You're supposed to be in your room!" he hissed. We had to whisper because everyone else was in the living room watching television and we didn't want to get caught red handed in the kitchen.

"I'm going to call a friend, now go away!"

"Sheesh, I just asked a simple question!" Mario Marco muttered as he walked away.

Finally I had some time to myself. I dialed and punched in a few numbers. After the ring tone, I got a chance to have an extremely short conversation. Syleria Susae thinks it was my fault the conversation ended up short because of me, but I think it was Sheryl Star who caused everything. If you didn't know, Sheryl Star is a Dalmatian from the Feline & K9 Companions with an owner named Sadie Dawes.

"Hello?"

"Hi, Sheryl Star, you can't believe this, but I have to stay in my room! Thanks to Mario Marco who got me in trouble, I am now grounded!"

"Oh."

"Also, have you heard about that unicorn in the county zoo?"

"Yeah, my family is trying to save money for admission tickets."

"WHAT?!?"

"What's the matter, Delilah Mara? Aren't you going too?"

"Well of course NOT! For your information, I don't believe in unicorns!"

"I didn't mean to upset you."

"You've already busted my bubble! How can you always believe everything you see on TV, on the radio, on the news, and practically EVERYWHERE? The world is practically lies, lies, lies if you asked me!"

I slammed down the phone on the receiver and stomped to my room. "This universe is SO unfair!" I thought. When I reached my room, I saw Mario Marco looking through MY SECRET NOTEBOOK! "What are you doing?" I yelled.

"I'm just looking."

"But it's supposed to be PRIVATE, meaning NO ONE else should READ it!"

"Well, I'm reading it now and I had found this in my dresser drawer."

"You did not! You're probably LYING!"

"No I'm not! Why don't you believe me?"

"Why should I? Give me my notebook back, NOW!"

Mario Marco refused and our argument got worse from there. Mario ripped a page out of my notebook and put it in his MOUTH! Seconds later, a gooey spitball came flying my way and I ducked as three more headed toward me. I rushed straight toward my opponent. He quickly moved out of my way and I ended up running into an open closet. My head hit a wall. "Ouch," I moaned. Clothes from a rack came rolling over me like an oversized avalanche. I screamed as I was buried in clothes. I coughed and gasped for breath.

I made my way out of the closet, but the bedroom door was open and Mario Marco was nowhere in sight! Golly, he must have run to hide! I could feel the hot steam rising out of my ears. I searched the kitchen, but no one was there. He couldn't be in the living room, because that's where Allie Angie, Gabriel Gordon,

Pierre, and Royal Romeo were watching television.

Quietly I crept into the bathroom. I heard some familiar giggling in the bathtub and automatically I saw my notebook on the edge of the bathtub. I moved closer with nervousness. The shower curtain swayed and moved. Obviously, Mario Marco was hiding behind the shower curtain. Ha, ha, he thinks he's so smart. He can't even keep his little mouth shut. This was it! I grabbed that notebook and zoomed out. I heard Mario Marco exclaim, "Hey!' and jump out of the bathtub. I didn't care. I just ran and ran. When I arrived back in the bedroom, I squeezed myself between a wall and the headboard of Mario Marco's bed. I knew he wouldn't find me. I made myself hidden just in time because at that moment, Mario Marco burst open the door shouting my name and looking for me. Immediately he went over to the open closet. I snuck out of my hiding place as he went deeper into the closet. As soon as he was out of view, I skipped on over and shut that closet door shut.

"Hey! Get me out of here!" cried Mario Marco. I locked the door and left my rival in the depths of the dark closet. I checked my notebook to see if it wasn't too bad in condition and shape. The pages were all wrinkled and wet with doggy drool. The front page had a huge rip and it looked like everything was falling apart! Oh no! Well, I'll get Mrs. Louis when she comes home and she'll deal with Mario.

Part III: Syleria Susae

We came back home and it looked like Mario Marco and Delilah Mara had gotten into another fight. What happened was that Mario Marco had stolen Delilah Mara's notebook and practically destroyed it. Mario Marco was spanked for what he did. His punishment was to stay in his room for another month and do household chores everyday for three weeks and write a one hundred word paper on how he could be an obedient puppy. I feel sorry for him in a way, but I could tell that everyone else was relieved. Mario Marco would have to work for Mrs. Louis to help earn money to buy Delilah Mara a new notebook. "You should know better than to look in something that doesn't belong to you," said Mrs. Louis. "But it said things about us, good and bad," Mario Marco complained. "It doesn't matter. You should not be spying on other people's possessions. Be glad Delilah Mara kept her thoughts to herself," our owner replied.

After dinner, I went on the internet to purchase admission tickets to the zoo. It seemed like we had saved a lot of money and because this was mostly my idea, Mrs. Louis gave me the honor of buying the tickets. I clicked and typed as I entered names, our address, credit card numbers, and any other identification information. I clicked the "submit" button and according to the shipping and handling schedules, the tickets should arrive in two days. Patience had also ordered her tickets on the same day, so we should receive them around the same time. I couldn't believe it! We were actually going to see a real, live, unicorn!

When Vanessa Pana and I discussed what we could do at the zoo, Delilah Mara started making fun of us. "You're just wasting money and time believing all this junk, why can't you do something better like raising money for a trip to Rome or Disneyworld?" she snapped.

Mrs. Louis made Delilah Mara mop and sweep the kitchen and that shut her up. In a couple of days, we would be at the zoo watching the exotic Juniper Jade do world famous tricks. Then Sophie would write her article and email it to the Weekly Junior News to be published.

I happily crawled into bed that night. I was so excited that I couldn't sleep. In a few days' time, the event would come and I just couldn't wait!

It was August 6th which was Sunday. Patience, Vanessa Pana, Sophie, and I decided to go over to the county library, the San Francisco Library of History.

Mrs. Louis dropped us off at four in the afternoon. As soon as we stepped in the library, we headed toward the fiction section. Right away we started searching for books on unicorns. So far these titles looked interesting:

Unicorn Myth & Magic
History of the Unicorn
Fairy Tales & Adventures of the Uni
Legends of the Unknown
Unicorn Breeds
Unicorn Beliefs & Criticism

In the end, we checked out these books and when we would arrive home, we would start reading instantly. We quickly glanced and read quotes, lines, and facts like "The unicorn is a rare creature. Though its similarities correspond with the mammal of a horse, it differs greatly in its former characteristics . . . On its forehead is a long, steel, horn full of power . . . They are solitary at times, but friendly creatures, usually in hiding. . . Many believe negatively about their existence . . . the book of Legends states such facts and events of those who have seen the unicorn for themselves. Sadly, humans have found no evidence."

In a section of the library was a table of computers. Anyone could use them to search on the internet. As it turned out, we shared two computers and the first thing we typed was "unicorn" and we hit the search button. Right away we received many results such as web pages about Juniper Jade and her fame which had not just spread across the country, but worldwide too. We printed about twenty seven pages about unicorns and nine about Juniper Jade. On our way out, the librarian stated, "You sure like unicorns don't you?" "It's for an article I'm writing and publishing for the Weekly Junior News," Sophie replied. The librarian lady awed in excitement, "How interesting! Well, have fun and we hope to see you again!"

We carried our books and information in a small cart and we waited on a nearby bench under an oak tree for Mrs. Louis to pick us up. If you didn't know, the library is in a nearby town, so we just passed the time by glancing up, down, all around our environment. Lots of cars were passing, honking, and parking. In just five minutes there was lots of traffic. People rode on bicycles or walked to nearby stores, buildings, and parlors. The weather seemed very warm with the sun shining and not a dark cloud was in sight. We relaxed and read more pages of our library books.

After several minutes, Mrs. Louis picked us up and we shopped around town. First we took a look around a women's bath and body works shop. We walked by walls that were stacked with bottles, perfumes, makeup, and containers. Patience sneezed a couple of times. Cats aren't so used to sweet smelling stuff, including perfumes.

As we explored a far end of the store, we looked up at a high rack full of UNICORN shampoos, make up, perfume, and purses on an expensive price of twenty dollars. After a couple more minutes of viewing more products, we went out of the shop and into a grocery store to buy some food. But just as we stepped into an aisle, we noticed products advertising UNICORNS! There were pictures of

Juniper Jade on milk cartons, cereal boxes, canned foods, wallpaper, balloons, make-up, toys, clothes, television sets, bicycles, sports gear, pet food packages, lottery machines, vending machines, medicine bottles, shopping carts, AND of course, the shopping bags. Practically everything had Juniper Jade on it!

"Whoa!" I exclaimed. "Look at all this unicorn stuff!" screamed Vanessa Pana with delight. For the next few minutes, we glanced around the store and all products were labeled with unicorns. "We might as well continue with our shopping," reminded Mrs. Louis. That snapped us out of our thoughts. Mrs. Louis showed us her shopping list:

1 carton of milk
3 boxes of cereal
2 bags of "Puppy Nip" treats
4 pairs of socks
6 rolls of toilet paper
1 dozen pack of eggs

It looked like this trip was going to be easy. We started searching for our requested items at once. Patience got us a carton of milk and smack on the front was a unicorn photo of Juniper Jade saying, "Take in calcium and vitamins and you can be healthy like me." Who knows if the unicorn really drinks milk? Vanessa Pana brought three boxes of three different brands of cereal: "K9 Krunchies," "Cheerios," and "Froot Loops." As usual, a label with a tiny picture of Juniper Jade was on the front stating, "Make a wish and it will come true." That was exactly what I was going to do. Well, not right now, but probably later. Next, we passed through the pet section where we collected two bags of treats. On the back of the bags was information on where you could order zoo tickets, the prices, and the location of the zoo. I gathered a pack of six rolls of toilet paper. But Mrs. Louis objected, "Syleria Susae, I think I asked for regular white colored rolls of toilet paper." I looked down at what I was holding and sure enough there were little unicorn designs all over every space of the paper.

"I think you're right, Mrs. Louis. I don't think the "guys" will like using this brand of toilet paper," Sophie agreed. By the word "guys" she meant Gabriel Gordon, Mario Marco, Royal Romeo, Pierre, and Mr. Louis.

They had already freaked out over a box of pink tissue paper and a blue baby hairbrush with teddy bear designs that we purchased from a drugstore a couple of weeks ago.

"But this is the only brand they're selling," I explained. "What?!? That can't be possible!" cried Mrs. Louis as she raced to an aisle stacked with shelves of unicorn toilet paper. "This is hopeless! What will everyone at home think?" I asked. "We'll just have to deal with this then. By the way, this is only toilet paper and it's not as if unicorns are really decorated ON our food. It's only on the boxes of cereal, bags of treats, and a carton that contains milk," Mrs. Louis declared.

"I'm afraid you're wrong," sighed Patience who had just fetched a package of eggs. According to Patience, the eggs had been painted with cute patterns of more unicorns! "Don't even think of trying to find white colored eggs. This is practically all they have," she added. We all stood speechless. Unicorns, unicorns, unicorns! That really was all this store was selling: UNICORNS! Furniture was engraved with unicorns. Barbie collections were releasing more unicorns and deserts like chocolate chip cookies, cinnamon rolls, and cakes were starting to look and become shaped like . . . unicorns! "I have had enough of this! I think we should go and shop at another store!" Sophie groaned. Mrs. Louis agreed to buy all her requested items except for the eggs. "They're probably other stores selling nice white cream colored eggs. It's not as if the whole world is unicorns," said Mrs. Louis.

At the cash register, we waited until our items were paid for and it looked like unicorns were all people seemed to talk about, including the employees of the store.

The magazines near the cash register advertised unicorns and even Hollywood has convinced their actors and singers to dress like unicorns. I didn't think this was "Uni-fever" as an actor had said in a magazine interview. I thought this was all just too corny!

We went out and visited another store that was a couple blocks away. You would have thought luck would have found us, but unusually it didn't. This store was completely empty and sold out of EVERYTHING because of unicorn advertisements. Mrs. Louis asked the store manager about the eggs, but he predicted that the store wouldn't sell regular colored eggs until the summer of next year! It looked like all stores across the world would do the same thing. "Forget the eggs! It's not as if we need them anyway! We can survive one perfect year without some scrambled eggs if we have to!" Mrs. Louis grumbled. I could tell she was really getting annoyed. Unicorns, unicorns, unicorns! All the world talks about is unicorns!

Part IV: Mario Marco

Mrs. Louis, Vanessa Pana, and Syleria Susae finally came home from their shopping. But it looks like they checked out some UNICORN library books! Isn't that crazy? But what was worse about this evening was that we weren't able to eat the egg casserole that Mrs. Louis planned to make for dinner because all the eggs in every store had unicorns. We decided to settle down for some cereal. Our club obviously ate K9 Krunchies.

I knew Juniper Jade was all over the cereal box, but I didn't expect unicorns to be IN our cereal. As I poured myself a bowl of cereal, I noticed some rainbow colored unicorn marshmallows! I would have rather preferred rainbow colored unicorn scrambled eggs than this!

"What in the world is THIS?!? If you're trying to convince me to believe that cone headed horse is actually a real unicorn, it's NOT going to work! Now give me some "real" cereal! This stuff tastes like pure sugar!" I shouted as I pounded my spoon on the table. "It's not anyone's fault, Mario. The stores all around the country are selling unicorn products," Mrs. Louis explained. I couldn't argue back and I just had to eat this squishy cereal that contained more marshmallows than what was really supposed to be inside.

After we ate dinner, we helped unpack the groceries that still lay untouched in their bags. As usual, some of us freaked out over the groceries. The carton of milk and bag of puppy treats didn't receive a lot of criticism, but when it came to the toilet paper, WOW, there were A LOT of complaints. The toilet paper was PINK and had little Juniper Jade unicorns. Boy was Mr. Louis mad! "I am NOT going to use "UNICORN" toilet paper! Never in MY life!" he yelled.

But Vanessa Pana and Syleria Susae had to explain to everyone that all stores across the country were selling unicorn merchandise. "I'd go around the globe, all the way to Asia, just to find some non unicorn food for once," Delilah Mara declared. "Don't feel distressed. In a few weeks this should all be over and our regular food will be out on sale again," Mrs. Louis reassured. "It had better be! Or I'll march straight toward the White House and demand for regular, non unicorn nutritious, natural food!" growled Royal Romeo. "This cereal is way too sugary for our anatomy. We could gain five extra pounds per day. I will NOT go out in public looking like a meatball!" added Gabriel Gordon. "I'll just use the restroom outside and build an outhouse. For toilet paper, we could use old magazines," Pierre suggested.

"Don't be ridiculous! We can get along just fine with unicorn merchandise," said Mrs. Louis calmly. "Unicorns, unicorns, unicorns! I could destroy ANYTHING that had to do with unicorns!" moaned Allie Angie.

"What about my pair of socks? Didn't you get those?" asked Mr. Louis. "I'm afraid not. All the clothes in the men's section were colored with blue and green unicorns. I saw a pair of yellow duck socks, but I didn't think you would like those," replied Mrs. Louis sadly. "I would have gladly had those instead," he sighed.

So let's say that dinnertime was really boring and out of our luck. When Mrs. Louis wasn't looking, Pierre would grab a big piece of construction paper and start making sketches of the outhouse he wanted to construct outside of the apartment. I went to bed late that night and while Delilah Mara helped with the dishes in the kitchen, I found out that she was still able to write stuff about us. Even though I had chewed up her notebook, she started scribbling down her thoughts on little scraps of paper she kept hidden under her bed mattress.

Earlier today, I had seen her writing on paper and stuffing it in her bed and that's when I became suspicious. I grabbed a few scraps of paper and started to read:

SYLERIA SUSAE IS A FANTASY FREAK

MARIO MARCO IS A BLOATED HOTDOG

ALLIE ANGIE LOOKS LIKE AN ABSURD ALIEN

VANESSA PANA IS A NO-NO NERD

GABRIEL GORDON IS TOO BRAINY; I
THINK HE'S GONE INSANEY!

PIERRE WASTES HIS TIME, ESPECIALLY
ON PLANNING THE OUTHOUSE.

ROYAL ROMEO TALKS TOO MUCH
SOMETIMES. IF HE TALKS FOR THREE
MONTHS STRAIGHT WITHOUT STOPPING,
I WOULDN'T WAIT UNTIL HIS BRAIN
CIRCUITS BLACKED OUT AND HIS HEAD
EXPLODED.

I quickly shoved the papers
under the mattress as I heard loud
footsteps. Luckily it was only
Mrs. Louis who came to give me the
list of chores I would need to
complete for tomorrow and how much
money I would earn if I completed
each and everyone of them:

        1 - VACCUM ALL ROOMS
        2 - MOP KITCHEN
        3 - SWEEP KITCHEN & BATHROOMS
        4 - CLEAN FURNITURE
        5 - ORGANIZE PANTRY &
        REFRIGERATOR

TOTAL OF MONEY EARNED: $0.25
Usually I don't get paid much
as you can see and a fancy
notebook, as Delilah Mara had

requested cost as much as SIX dollars!!! This sure is going to take a while, probably about a month to earn all this money! What's bad enough is that the stuff in the pantry and kitchen usually end up out of order even if you organize everything. No one seemed to care to place things where they should belong. We have so much stuff in the pantry that when it's piled up on shelves and racks, you can't seem to open the pantry door without getting buried in an avalanche. If only Delilah wasn't around, maybe this would be a lot easier.

Part V: Allie Angie

Today was Monday, August 7th around 9a.m. I just had some more of that disgusting cereal and this was a chance to get the taste off of my taste buds. Because I was the first one finished eating, I got a chance to watch some television. But here's what happened every time I changed channels:

"Buy your unicorn food here at Meijer."
Click.

"See the ultimate unicorn cotton candy maker!"
  Click.
"Get your zoo tickets & season passes today!"
  Click.
"All hail Queen Juniper Jade!"
  Click.
"Dashing through the snow, on a one unicorn sleigh, over the hills we go, wishing all the way . . ."
  Click
"Unicorn books and CD's on a special offer."
  Click.

"Hey, go back to the last channel!" Syleria Susae shouted.

"Fine. I don't really want to watch TV anyway," I said glumly. When the channel changed, I heard a television announcer shout, "Get your unicorn books for an extremely low price and help yourself to some unicorn music CDs, cassettes, and records! Buy two; get one free only at Barnes & Nobles Booksellers!" Vanessa Pana quickly turned off the TV and rushed into the kitchen asking Mrs. Louis if she, Syleria Susae, and possibly Patience could go to the bookstore and buy some unicorn products. Obviously, Mrs. Louis agreed and phoned the LeLaine Residence and received a positive reply. It was now settled. Patience, Syleria Susae, and Vanessa Pana would set out on another unicorn tour. When was this ever going to stop? I think the country is getting too carried away over a white painted horse with a wig and a fake horn.

I marched straight toward my room to write a complaint to the president:

Dear Mr. President,
I demand non-unicorn products to be sold at stores and for the burning of all books and music that have anything to do with unicorns!

I immediately stopped. "This is useless!" I yelled as I crumpled my paper and threw it across the room. Unfortunately, it flew into an open bathroom door and into the TOILET!

I'd better get that paper out before Mrs. Louis notices. I don't want to flush the toilet and clog the bathroom pipes. All because of

ONE paper, we would have to summon a plumber. We might as well be safe than sorry.

Later around four o' clock, Syleria Susae and Vanessa Pana got back from the bookstore with bags of books and CDs. I glanced at some CD titles and they sure were weird:

-Uni Puni by Aly & A.J.
-Magical Myth by Shakira
-Make a Wish by Jesse McCartney
-Some Unicorns Are Evil by Michael Jackson
-Power of the Horn by Raven Symone
-It's More Than Just Once Upon A Time by Spice Girls
-Fly Away by Britney Spears
-Unicorns on Valentine's Day by Christina Aguilera

I could hardly pronounce the names of the book titles they checked out like, "Unidrasticalimanuelmania," "Mythmenticallyfaithfilledhistoric althemes," and "Legendarycalifragilisticcriticalf antasyfacts." Have a nice day reading those unintelligent books. Maybe I could listen to some of the music, but the books just seem too unpredictable. Tomorrow quickly came and it was August 8th, Tuesday. Another boring morning had come, but that's not all.

The zoo tickets arrived in the mailbox at noon and sure enough Syleria Susae and Vanessa Pana shot out of the front door like cannons on Bunker Hill a second right after the mailman had come into the apartment lobby. Two walls of the lobby have everyone's mailboxes. The mailboxes looked like mini lockers and you had to memorize the combination of your mailbox. In less than ten seconds, they zoomed right back shouting, "We got the zoo tickets! Yea!"

Again Mrs. Louis phoned the LeLaine Residence and surprisingly Patience, Sophie, and Mrs. LeLaine got their tickets too! That evening, during dinner, Mrs. Louis announced that the zoo trip was going to be tomorrow! I nearly fell out of my chair when she said it. "Mario Marco, Delilah Mara, don't forget to do your chores! Gabriel Gordon, Royal Romeo, remember to run by the grocery

store with Mr. Louis!" she
reminded.

   If you didn't know, our next
door neighbors moved out and now
we live together in the same
apartment. It was a little bad for
Mrs. Louis because she now has a
total of EIGHT puppies to care
for. Mrs. Louis continued, "Allie
Angie, don't make any messes in
the kitchen. Everyone, I hope you
keep the house clean!" I think
everything would have gone fine if
Mario Marco hadn't said, "And
Delilah Mara, I hope you don't
throw the dishes across the table
or flood the washer with detergent
that made our clothes turn green
like you almost did last time."
"Whatdya mean, oversized
meatball?" she remarked. "I mean
you, you warted canine toad!" he
argued. "Please settle down right
now!" Mrs. Louis commanded. But
the fighting still continued:

   "Mara of the Mocking!"
   "Brown Baloney Ball!"
   "Ugly Loser of Death"
   "Absurd Ant of Evil!''
   "Banana Booger Brain!"
   "Oatmeal Face!"
   "Fish Lips!"

"Spaghetti Sauce Slime!"

"Miss 5,000 ton Gordo Girl!"

"Nincompoop!"

"Mr. Gigundo Poodle-made Football!"

"White Ghastly Witch of Oz!"

"Dummy Duck!"

"Dweeby Dufus!"

"Big, fat, stinky, baby goose, fat beaked, monster!"

Mario Marco and Delilah Mara hopped on the dinner table and started throwing food at each other. Mr. Louis tried to settle down Delilah. But it seemed like nothing really helped. Gabriel Gordon quickly came up with an idea. He rushed into the garage and brought a chain and a rope. As you would expect, we tied Delilah Mara to the living room sofa and Mario Marco to a wall. That finally brought peace to our innocent household.

Part VI: Syleria Susae

It's August 9th, Wednesday. It was seven twenty three in the morning and I was up for a day's adventure. I spent the next fifthteen minutes grooming myself and almost half an hour deciding on what I should bring like cameras to take pictures and paper to list notes about the unicorn. I came down early for breakfast, but surprisingly, Vanessa Pana was already eating some unicorn marshmallow cereal with unicorn shaped toast. On the kitchen counter, was a little radio that played unicorn music. Mrs. Louis arrived to eat her meal ten minutes later. We gobbled up our food and hopped in our car and drove over to Patience's house. Just as we stopped in front of her house, the garage door opened and out came our three friends. We greeted each other and we got in separate vehicles. About twenty minutes later, we entered the zoo's parking lot to see HUNDREDS and possibly THOUSANDS of cars! It took practically forever to find a parking space. We jumped out of our cars and scurried past trucks and mini vans. When we reached the zoo entrance, lines were packed full of people. After ten minutes, we showed our tickets and we were let into the zoo. Right away Mrs. LeLaine picked up a copy of the zoo's map. "Just in case we get lost," she reminded.

It was hard making our way to the unicorn show ring, the place where Juniper Jade was being shown. I got lost a couple of times and it took quite a while to use the restroom because ALL of the bathrooms in the zoo seemed to be packed full EVERY second! EVERY moment a few people would go in the restroom while two or three may come out. A disaster eventually hit.

While we were waiting for some empty stalls, I heard a lady scream and rush out of a stall. People crowded around to see what was happening and the stall's toilet started to shake rapidly and bubble up. Seconds later, gushes of water squirted and toxic waste out of the toilet and water kept flushing in the toilet bowl. Other people screamed started dashing out of the restroom.

Another lady fought her way through the rushing people to the broken toilet. She pushed the toilet handle and the toilet started to run like normal. "Whew!" she sighed. But some of the people watching started to gasp as ALL of the water immediately disappeared down the toilet. "Well, this is nice! A toilet with no water!" a little girl complained. "That's peculiar," wondered the lady who took a closer look in the toilet bowl to see why the water had gone away, but then all of a sudden . . . a spray of "brown" gushy stuff shot out of the toilet and onto the lady's face and clothes. She yelled and ran off in horror screaming, "Ew! Get this stuff off of me!"

Everyone left in the bathroom started to back away from the stall. But it was tool late. The toilet shook and the toilet handle just FELL right off! Then the toilet EXPLODED and the walls of the stall started to crack! It was a good thing I wasn't in front of the crowd because I might have gotten a spray of "toxic" waste. Mrs. Louis and Mrs. LeLaine hurried us out of there and we made our way to the unicorn show ring.

If you didn't know, the unicorn show ring was a big, and I mean REALLY big tent that looked like something from a circus. It was white with little Juniper Jade unicorns. As we approached closer and closer, I was able to see the tent's entrance with a very long line with MANY people. "This is probably going to take a while," said Sophie as she started to count the people. This is what our conversation sounded like:

Patience – "How long do you think this will take?"

Sophie – "23 . . . 36 . . . 41. . ."

Vanessa – "No idea."

Sophie – "52 . . . 62 . . . 77 . . ."

Mrs. LeLaine – "I can't seem to find any good clothes for Sophie when she goes back to school!"

Sophie – "81 . . . 85 . . . 88 . . ."

Mrs. Louis – "I know what you mean."

Sophie – "92 . . . 97 . . . 103 . . ."

Mrs. LeLaine – "Every clothes company keeps on selecting unicorns for their main clothes designs."

Sophie– "105 . . . 109 . . . 114 . . ."

Mrs. LeLaine – "Well at least I do. I mean, if that unicorn was truly real, it wouldn't just be shown at a common zoo and the world would practically be covered with unicorns!"

Sophie- "144 . . . 148 . . . 156 . . ."

Mrs. Louis - "Sort of like it is in our country now, I guess."

Sophie- "173 . . . 177 . . . 180 . . ."

Mrs. LeLaine - "You sure got me there."

10 minutes later

Sophie-"2148 . . 2156 . . 2159 . . . ."

Vanessa Pana - "It would be cool if we saw more of the Feline & K9 Companions. If they were here, maybe they could help us solve the mystery of Juniper Jade."

Sophie-"2182 . . 2189 . . . 2195 . . ."

Patience - "What about Sheryl Star?"

Sophie-"2207 . . 2215 . . . 2219 . . ."

Vanessa Pana - "That would really help us."

Sophie-"2227 . . 2238 . . . 2247 . . ."

Patience - "No, Vanessa! I mean they're here!"
Sophie - "Stop shouting, I'll have to start all over again if you don't stop and I've already counted more than 2,000 people in TEN WHOLE minutes! 2251 . . . 2263 . . ."

Patience pointed ahead and among the crowds of people were the Dawes family with Sheryl Star, Panda Perry, Rosie, and Halloween.

Vanessa Pana - "Come on, everyone! Let's go and meet them!"

So we rushed ahead to meet more members of the famous national detective agents, the Feline & K9 Companions. Also, Vanessa Pana really has an interest for Jackson, Sadie Dawes's white standard poodle. She doesn't have a crush on him or anything, but she just adores his intelligence. As soon as we made our way to our new friends, Patience gladly introduced us.

Patience - "Hi guys, glad to see that you stopped by to see the unicorn!"
Sheryl Star - "Hey, Pate! Long time, no see!"

Patience - "Meet my friends, Vanessa Pana and Syleria Susae."

As Mrs. LeLaine, Mrs. Louis, and Mrs. Dawes chatted away, Sophie discussed the ideas of her article. What surprised me was that Sheryl Star and her feline friends wanted to help!

Rosie - "Why don't you write a list to summarize your article?"

Halloween - "Yeah! Let's start a list of some important information you may want to know."

Panda Perry - "Are you ready to start writing?"

Sophie - "I'm better than ready!" Sophie's notepad ended up looking like this:

We need: -fur color -eye color - body color

-Color of horn -Special markings?
-Name -Age
-D.O.B. -Gender -Favorite food? - Favorite food?

About half an hour later, we were in our seats and before our eyes were a huge circus arena decorated with unicorn flags and streamers. On the floor of the arena, were hoops, stools, mats, trampolines, and even a balance beam! This looked very much like a circus! But where was the unicorn?

Our question was answered when a ringmaster dressed in a black suit came to start our show. "Good day, ladies and gentleman! Welcome to the San Francisco Zoo where we shall be presenting our main attraction: Juniper Jade the Unicorn of Joy and Truth!" he announced. Then a flash of light and shower of heavy streamers, we saw a unicorn shaped figure trotting gallantly toward the arena. As soon as all of the streamers and glitter vanished, we saw the most amazing animal in the world!

Juniper Jade whinnied and shook her dazzling mane. Her horn glowed and shone bright in the light of the arena. The crowd rose and started to shout and cheer in awe. That's when the show began to start. A horse trainer who was dressed in a clown outfit led the unicorn around the arena. Juniper Jade showed off her talent with many tricks. She hopped form stool to stool and jumped through a hoop of fire. Next, she bounced up and down on a trampoline and rode on an elephant! Rock music played over some speakers and Jade tapped and danced to the music on boots and later on skates! She even did courageous flips on the balance beam!

When half of the show passed, Juniper Jade prepared to do her final act. She bravely went up some steps near the ceiling to a small platform. I hadn't noticed this before, but high up near the platform was a tightrope! The crowd gasped in horror while the unicorn took her first step on the black wired rope.

Vanessa Pana - "I'm scared!"
Sophie - "I can't watch!'
Mrs. LeLaine - "Don't worry, this is the circus. NO mistakes happen in a circus."
Sheryl Star - "I'm not so sure about that."

The unicorn's body swayed back and forth as she tried to balance on the small and thin rope. People started to scream and even cry! The unicorn slowly tiptoed to the other side of the rope. But just as soon as she was about to set a hoof on the platform on the opposite side of where she first started, the rope snapped! I closed my eyes and heard more shouting from the crowd. Rosie and Patience both started to yell in fear. But seconds later, the crowd started cheering! If they're happy that the unicorn is dead, then I'm insane, retarded, or crazy.

I opened one eye and spotted Juniper Jade on the platform safe and sound. From what I heard, it looked like Jade had leapt to the platform just in time! The horse trainer appeared in the arena again after Juniper Jade made her way off the platform and down some stairs.

"Our show is almost over, but we hope you had a magnificent time!" he stated. The crowd automatically went wild! "But we have one more act to show you which will include anyone who wants to participate!" he continued. Then he began to explain, "You ask the unicorn to dance to a certain music genre!" Immediately the crowd started to get noisy and it took a while for everyone to get quiet again. The horse trainer was able to give out instructions and everybody ended up forming a long line. Some people requested rock, pop, disco,

blues, soul, and even classical.
Every few minutes, a new kind of
music would play over the speakers
and the unicorn would dance around
in a ballerina outfit.

In forty minutes, the unicorn
was tired out and many people were
leaving. These were some of the
genres WE requested:
Mrs. LeLaine - Classical
Mrs. Louis - Hip Hop
Mrs. Dawes - Soul R & B
Syleria Susae - Rock
Vanessa Pana - Pop
Patience - Blues
Sophie - Country
Sheryl Star - Jazz
Halloween - Rap
Panda Perry - Rock
Rosie - Disco

But just as the unicorn and
the horse trainer were about to
leave, Sophie ran up to him
calling, "Sir, excuse me, but I'm
writing an article for a kids
magazine and I want to ask you
some questions about Juniper."
"Oh, I don't know. I have A LOT of
things to take care of today and I
need to take care of today and I
need to get a head start on
teaching Juniper some more

tricks," replied the horse trainer. "Please, it's urgent! It should only take a few minutes," Sophie pleaded. "All right, we really need more people to learn more about our unicorn and if it's for a kids magazine, you say, it's probably good to make this educational. First, I'll introduce myself. My name is Matthew Snicket, a friend of Robert Portman, the man who found Juniper Jade in Europe," he explained. After five minutes of interviewing, Sophie's notepad had all the answers to her questions:

-Horse trainer: Matthew Snicket
-Horse Owner: Robert Portman
-Fur Color: Strawberry
-Eye Color: Gold
-Body Color: White
-Color of Horn: Gold
-Special Markings? None
-Name: Juniper Jade
-Age: 3 years
-D.O.B: 2003
-Gender: F
-Favorite Foods: ice cream, cookies, strawberries, fruit snacks, donuts.

-Favorite Hobby: Granting wishes, performing, and making new friends.
-Any other info? None

Matthew gave Sophie a card with his phone number and Robert Portman's email. "It's very disappointing to say, but Mr. Portman never wants others to know his phone number because you can also find the address in the phone book. So he prefers to communicate by email," he explained. Matthew granted Sophie and her friends' permission to see the unicorn ONLY for interviewing.

On the car ride home, Patience and I chatted away about how they enjoyed the visit to the zoo. Vanessa Pana seemed extra curious about Sophie's interview with the horse trainer. She even took a really close look at every single bit of information on Sophie's notepad. "Were you nervous?" she asked. "Not really, I was kind of excited. But the good news is, this information should help me get a good start on that article I'll be writing," Sophie replied.

After that, we spent the rest of the car ride looking at our unicorn merchandise we had bought at the zoo. Mrs. Louis and Mrs. LeLaine both wore caps with unicorns on them and Sophie wore a jeweled necklace with a unicorn tag. Patience got a stuffed animal unicorn and Vanessa Pana and I wore sweatshirts that said: We Luv Unicorns! So as you can see, our days have been quite a unicorn craze.

Chapter 5: Circus Craze

It was August 10th, Thursday and the time was around eight in the morning. I was up and awake eating more unicorn marshmallow cereal and listening to more fantasy music on my unicorn mp3 player. I was so busy listening and eating that I didn't realize that the phone was ringing. Mrs. Louis quickly came downstairs in her pajamas and unicorn fuzzy slippers. She removed the headphones off my ears saying, "I think that's enough music for now, Syleria. You've been listening ever since last night. By the way, you've received a phone call from the Dawes Family."

I rushed to the phone and sure enough, Sheryl Star had left a message. I knew it wasn't for me, but I was eager to hear who it was for, anyway. It sounded something like this:

"This is a message for Delilah Mara. Delilah, this is Sheryl Star. You've got to learn to grow up for once. I know why you've stopped emailing me and it's all because I believe in that unicorn.

It's MY decision, Delilah. NOT yours! If you don't apologize, I won't be your friend ever again! You hear me? NEVER! I can believe in anything I want to believe in! Why are you acting this way? If you're going through some sort of problem, I could help. But I still don't get why you're so mad over something really absurd. Well, I've gotta go. See ya."

Okay, that was IT! Delilah Mara is getting out of hand. I marched toward her room where she was still all sound asleep. "WAKE UP!!!" I yelled. Delilah jumped up and by accident, rolled off the bed with a tremendous thud. The whole room shook and a nearby shelf that contained books fell to the ground. That wasn't all. Picture frames on the wall cracked and slipped off to be found in glass shatters on Mrs. Louis's new rug which was also drenched in a chemical formula that had been on a nearby desk. I could tell that Gabriel Gordon wouldn't be happy to see that the formula he had been working on for weeks would be ruined.

The red rug was turning green and bubbly as the formula soaked into the fabric. Delilah seemed quite dazed as she bumped her head on a chair which had Pierre's bug collection. The container with the bugs shook and toppled over, on top of Delilah. You'd think not much would have happened, but the lid of the square shaped container snapped off and a total of seventy three insects and other creatures poured out. Pretty soon, Delilah was covered in beetles, flies, roaches, ants, centipedes, spiders, and many more types of insects. She screamed, "What's going on?!?" Delilah looked up at me and narrowed her eyes with a growl that made my teeth chatter.

Mrs. Louis, Gabriel Gordon, Pierre, Mario Marco, and Vanessa Pana came to see what the fuss was all about and I could tell that they were NOT pleased. Gabriel Gordon still had his pajamas on, Pierre's fur was not brushed, Mario Marco's mouth was covered in toothpaste, Vanessa Pana was in her pink pony slippers, and Mrs. Louis had hot chocolate stains all over her bathrobe.

"What's happened here?" asked Mrs. Louis worriedly looking around the messed up room. "My new rug is ruined!" gasped Mrs. Louis as she realized that her brand new rug had turned a disgusting, fungus, green. "My bug collection!" yelped Pierre. The bugs had already crawled from Delilah to all corners of the bedroom. "Is that my chemical formula?" asked Gabriel Gordon who eyed the rug suspiciously. "I worked hard trying to rearrange my calculations and research on my results! It took four whole weeks to construct this new element!" he continued sadly.

When Vanessa Pana saw the shattered photo frames, she immediately burst in tears saying, "I spent my whole allowance on those expensive frames and now thirty dollars has gone to waste!" The books from the shelf had also ripped pages and torn book covers. Mario Marco's face turned bright red and he had a straight faced expression. "I checked these books out of the library and now I'm gonna probably be charged with a large fine," he grumbled. "Who started all this?" asked Mrs. Louis sternly.

I explained how I just wanted to let Delilah know that Sheryl Star had left a message on the phone. Delilah was a heavy sleeper, so hollering was practically the only option I had to wake her up. "I see now that it was an accident, but you have to be careful next time. Syleria, you will have to give us each ten dollars from your allowance to help us repair or replace things that are ruined," said Mrs. Louis. "Also, you may want to take a trip to the store to buy cream and medicine for Delilah," she reminded. Now that she mentioned it, I noticed Delilah's skin turning red, black, and blue from the bumps and bite marks forming all over her body.

Delilah was busily scratching away and every second, her bug bites grew more and more rashed up and infected. I gave Delilah the phone so she could hear Sheryl's message. After she heard the whole message, she burst in great anger. "Let her be that way! Why should I care?" she snapped. I tried telling Delilah that everyone has their own right to believe in anything they want, even unicorns. But by the way she rolled her eyes and pretended to yawn; I could tell that she didn't want to listen.

When I was finished talking, I saw that my lecture hadn't worked and she wasn't the least bit convinced. Instead of confessing and apologizing for her attitude, she yelled, "When are you gonna run to the store to get my medicine? These bug bites are more than irritating, you know. Are you gonna hand me my ten dollars? Where's the respect I'm supposed to get? Don't tell me that you forgot because I am NOT gonna remind you." Before I knew it, Delilah had lifted up my ear and complained, "I want what I deserve and I want it NOW!!!" Ouch. Ouch. And double ouch. I think I'm gonna go deaf any second. What Delilah deserved was a kick in the butt, but I didn't say so, or else I might really go deaf!

I continued on my way. I paid my friends and Mrs. Louis, and got ready to go to the grocery store. At the store, I passed an aisle with my wagon, and my cellphone rang. I had to use a wagon for my shopping because a shopping cart was way too BIG. It turned out that Sophie was calling!

"Hey Syleria, whatz up?"
"Uh, fine. I'm doing a little bit of shopping right now."
"Sorry to barge in like this, but I have wonderful news!"
"Let me guess, you got a postcard from the unicorn."
"No, Susae. I typed my article for the Junior Magazine!"
"Really?"
"Yeah! By email, I sent it to the magazine company and the published article will be in the next magazine that's going to be issued tomorrow. EVERYONE in the state will get a magazine copy in the mail!"
"Whoa. That's like so totally awesome!"
"Also, don't forget to buy a newspaper on your way out of the store."
"Why?"
"There's a page that announces that Juniper Jade will be showing at the Los Angeles Circus!"

"WOW!"

"I know, isn't it great? Patience and I are going to the library to check out some books on circuses. Do you wanna come?"

"I can't. I have A LOT to do today and I'm sure Mrs. Louis wants me to run some errands."

"Ok. Patience and I will try to find some books for you."

"Thank you! Bye!"

I hung up and continued with my shopping. I ventured through an aisle with medicine and first aid kits. I checked out brands of medicines, but nothing seemed to have the right cure for any of Delilah's symptoms. I was just about to give up, but on a high shelf were bottles of brands of medicines for bug bites. The medicine was in the form of pills, liquids, creams, and even powder! I snatched four medicine bottles and continued on my way to the cash register. I paid only TEN dollars for the medicine and seventy five cents for a newspaper. The medicine seemed to be past the expiration date, but who cares? They were in the store and on sale AND I wanted to get this over with.

When I got home, I watched as Delilah Mara took three pills, four teaspoons of medicine, some cream on her bug bites, and powder in iced tea. Mrs. Louis tucked Delilah Mara into bed so she could rest while I spent the rest of the day writing Delilah, Pierre, Gabriel, Mario, Vanessa, and Mrs. Louis apology letters that had to be FOUR HUNDRED words long!!! I took a piece of paper and scribbled:

Dear Delilah Mara, SORRY!!!!!!!!!!!!!! Now are ya happy? This is YOUR fault, NOT mine!

P.S. Don't be a heavy sleeper, or else you ruin everything, you deranged, mutant, overweight, Mocking Mara, quack!

I wish I could give this to Delilah, but I knew that this was quite a short letter. I really wanted to get this over with, but how? I sat at a desk eating away at my eraser. "This might take a while," I thought.

Part VII: Patience

It was noon and Sophie and I were on our way to the library. We

had finished our chores and Sophie
sent her article by email to the
magazine company. With me as her
editor, her article would be in
tip top shape and hopefully be
approved by the magazine company.
Now that our work was finished for
today, we had the rest of the
hours free to take a visit to the
library! Earlier today, Sophie had
checked the mail and found out
that Juniper Jade would be shown
at a circus in Los Angeles.
Because I had been so curious and
full of questions, Sophie got the
hint that I wanted to go to the
library to find out more on
circuses.

     We set out on another
adventure hoping to find something
new. I was in the library in no
time and already looking for
circus books. But surprisingly,
there were LOTS of people. It
seemed like everyone was in one
particular section of the library.
The crowd was so thick that an
enormous cloud of dust had formed.
As soon as the mass of people
left, we saw empty bookshelves
that had once contained books,
magazines, and encyclopedias about
circuses. "Maybe it wasn't such a

good idea to come to the library,'' said Sophie. "I think we should have come earlier," I added. "Why don't we ask the librarian why ALL these books were checked out all of a sudden?" I quickly suggested. "Great idea, I really want to know what's going on," Sophie agreed. We made our way to the check out counter where a LONG line of people were waiting to check out their books. It looked like these people were high schoolers. But either way, each person had from three to a maximum total of fifthteen books!

Most of the books were the books from the Circus Section. With enough effort, Sophie and I pushed our way through the lines of people to the counter. I looked up and a librarian with puffy black hair, green eyes, and glasses faced me. "How may I help you?" she asked. "What happened to the circus books?" asked Sophie intently. "High school students from Westside Academy are checking them out for a special purpose," she replied.

If you didn't know, Westside Academy is a high school for smart kids. Usually students who have a B- or lower in ANY of their course subjects get suspended. The school tuition is a thousand dollars per month and only rich families seem to afford this type of payment nowadays. The school system is extremely strict and all students have to wear matching uniforms. What's worse is that school starts on the first day of August and ends in the middle of June, so there's not much of a vacation. Sophie's mother despises the school because she thinks all kids deserve a FULL summer vacation no matter how rich or intelligent those students may be.

"Our teacher assigned us a project. We need to write a five hundred word report on circuses, draw a photo of a circus, and research on each thing that may be included in a circus performance," explained a female red headed high school student. "Well, that explains the answer to your question. Everyone in Westside Academy must have been assigned the same project," the librarian concluded. Sophie let out a long sigh and then the next moment, I found myself walking glumly out of the library.

"So much for that," I muttered. "Don't be sad, Pate. We could always search through the internet and find websites on circuses," Sophie reassured. That made me feel a whole lot better. But our luck turned upside down as soon as Sophie typed in our keyword that revealed a list of unusual and unhelpful websites. Websites like "circuscraze.com," "Who Needs the Circus?.Html," "www.http://Stump the Seals OR Fire the Ringmaster.net, or "The Dumbest Entertainment.Org" didn't really seem to give us the information we needed. "This is SO boring! Why don't we just give up?" I cried. That's exactly what we did.

But later on after supper, Sophie must have told her father about how disappointed I was because he suggested that he'd take Sophie and I, and possibly Vanessa Pana and Syleria Susae to the Los Angeles Circus! Right away he phoned the Louis Family and returned home with a GOOD and BAD report: "It looks like Vanessa Pana can come along with us, but Mrs. Louis said Syleria Susae is grounded and she won't be able to join us." I gasped, "Why not?" "I am not sure. You may want to find out if you're curious," he told me. I rushed straight to our computer, logged onto my account, and prepared to send an email:

Dear Syleria,
What is wrong? Vanessa Pana can come to the circus with us, but you can't. Why not?
    Meow, Patience

    In a few minutes, after I sent my email, I received an unread message from Susae. Her message explained how she got in trouble and was the cause of a big accident that had to do with Delilah Mara, Mrs. Louis's new rug, Pierre's bug collection, Gabriel Gordon's chemical formula, Vanessa Pana's picture frames, and torn books that Mario Marco had checked out from the library. By the time I read the entire email, I burst in laughter. Sophie came to see what was so funny and in the end she was laughing too.

Part VIII: Syleria Susae

It was supper time and believe me, I wasn't happy. I was stuck in the house grounded because of the accident that happened this morning. I still had those apology letters to write, but so far I had thought of ONE sentence that said, "I'm Sorry." I'm horrible when it comes to writing and I guess this was the time when I could actually work on improving it. Like Mrs. Louis had said, "It builds character."

If you thought this morning had gone wrong, you should have seen what happened during dinner when we all sat quietly in our places at the table. Mrs. Louis served us soup and vegetables. I HATE vegetables! Usually I prefer lamb chops or a beef sandwich, but NO! We were forced to eat overheated lava looking carrots that melted in your mouth and made your tongue turn orange, smelly onions that made me cry all the time, broccoli that was so paste like, it practically turned my teeth green, and worst of all was desert, which tasted like salt, seafood, and barf! I thought this was all gonna make me hurl!

It was hard for me to believe that Mr. and Mrs. Louis were happily enjoying this weird "stuff," anyway. Mario Marco was messily eating his soup and Royal Romeo burped so loud that the room echoed and our dishes rattled. I glanced over and saw that Pierre was conducting a new recipe: He mixed his food by pouring his orange juice into his vegetable soup and Gabriel Gordon had decided to reheat his carrots in the microwave. By the time, the microwave timer dinged and he took his food out, the carrots were like mush and they left a hot, rotten vegetable odor floating around in the dining room. Boys can be so gross sometimes! I looked over and saw that Vanessa Pana's face had turned green and Allie Angie, who was sitting right beside her, did nothing but stare at her veggies and wish that she could rush out of the dining room and into the kitchen to munch on something more edible. But Delilah Mara looked as weird as ever. Her bug bites had turned green, white, and orange, just like the

VEGETABLES! I couldn't take this any longer!

Immediately I yelled, "Why are we eating this junk? Can't we at least eat something OTHER than vegetables? Where's the lamb chops? What about the turkey sandwiches and beef loaf? I don't get it!" Everyone stared at me with blank expressions except Royal Romeo who gave one last burp that made my cup shake and tip over, making orange juice spill all over my carrots. "Vegetables are healthy for dogs with bug bites," explained Mrs. Louis. "I know Delilah Mara has a case of bug bites, but it doesn't mean we ALL have to eat the same food, right?" I argued. "It sure saves humiliation! I mean, what do you want me to do? Enjoy eating vegetables with great depression while you ALL sit around me eating MEAT? I think it's no fair! EVERYONE should eat the same thing! If it wasn't for you, maybe all this would NOT have happened!" Delilah Mara muttered. I sat back down and Mrs. Louis finally added, "That shows a little more respect. Delilah Mara is ill and she must be treated with respect like any other princess in England would be treated." What in the world? It's like as if Mrs. Louis has joined Delilah's side or something! "WHAT?!? Delilah's no princess! She's just a common poodle with bug bites eating veggies at a dinner table! You call that royalty?!? I'm TIRED of eating this stuff!" I complained. "Go to your room, NOW!" demanded Mrs. Louis. "Yeah!" cheered the whole club, including Mr. Louis. "Fine!" I shouted. If everyone turns their back on me, I'll turn my back on them!

Chapter 6: The Wonder Unicorn

Today was Friday, August 11th. My morning was unusually quiet, but after I trudged all the way to the dining room for breakfast, everyone and everything seemed totally opposite. Usually I'm the first one ready to eat, but surprisingly my friends and owners were already halfway in the middle of their meal eating lettuce in soymilk! It looked similar to cereal, but in a more veggie like way. For desert, there were mashed potatoes mixed in gravy. We had that for dinner desert last night and believe me, it tasted HORRIBLE! The gravy was THREE weeks past the expiration date and the potatoes were pitch BLACK! It wasn't because they were rotten or anything, though.

Mrs. Louis told me that sometimes in the summer, farmers leave their potatoes out in the sun to get heated and they had a more unique taste if they were black! By the way she said it, I wasn't so sure if that was true or not. Then Delilah Mara told me that potatoes came out black because earthworms throw up on the potatoes and their vomit is black because of the soil they eat. Now that made my stomach twist and churn and I could feel my face turning green. Was I REALLY about to eat EARTHWORM BARF?!? I had NO IDEA! After that, Vanessa Pana said, "Those potatoes are rotten. But don't worry! They're especially good for you." When she left me, Pierre whispered in my ear, "Those potatoes aren't rotten. They are fresh and nutritious, now that they're covered in squashed flies." Oh my goodness! What was wrong with these potatoes anyway? Who should I believe? I had no clue! "Don't believe any of them, Susae. Those potatoes overheated on the stove and they sort of blacked out. So don't be surprised if they blacked out and taste crisp like something out of a barbecue," Mario Marco reassured. Ok, so maybe breakfast wasn't TOO bad, but I think the rest of the day just blew me off!

Right after I was finished eating, Delilah Mara took her medicine. But after she swallowed her last pill, I could tell that something went WRONG! Her fur turned completely rainbow colored and her bug bites swelled and grew larger about the size of golf balls, which made it look like she had boils or extra inflamed mosquito bites. Plus, her eyes turned red and so did her nose and her whole body seemed to swell and puff up all purple, black, and green. Delilah looked so messed up, I could barely recognize her. "Do you think these bug bites have finally gone away by now? It's been quite a while since I've been my normal self," she said. I was too speechless to answer her question, and all I did was STARE real hard at her unusual transformation.

"What are you lookin' at?" she growled. "I don't mean to make fun of you or anything, but I think you'd better take a look at yourself in the bathroom mirror," I suggested. Delilah walked off in a careless way.

"I've been insulted! I just know it!"

"I don't think so."

"Yeah right, Syleria. You're just making me feel like a dork. I bet

I'll walk through this bathroom door and see nothing but bug bites when I see my reflection in that mirror."

"Don't be so sure."
"You can quit joking, Susae."
"I'll probably be lucky to see no bug bites at all and my skin will be back to normal and . . . AHH!"

I heard running footsteps as everyone rushed to the bathroom to see what all the noise was all about. But everything sounded so confusing like this:

"Delilah, what happened?"
"You're growing golf ball bites!"
"Did you dye your hair or what?'
"Did you eat Delilah, you rainbow colored golf ball witch? You can't fool me with that disguise!"
"Help! Why do I look like this?!?"
"Call the police!"
"No way! We need the FBI!"
"Delilah looks C-O-O-L!"
"You think I look cool, Mr. Banana Brain?!? You look like an unfinished hamburger with only a bun and ketchup!"
"Everyone calm down!"

This went on and on and I put on a pair of earmuffs to block out the noise. I went outside for a nice walk to get some fresh air and then I walked back to my room to rest. But surprisingly, a piece of paper was on my bed which read: CONFIDENTIAL! TO SYLERIA SUSAE ONLY!!!

I opened up and note which said:
J is for jumping off a cliff
U is for the unicorn that falls
N is for NO! As in, there are NO such things as unicorns!
I stands for "I will destroy all unicorns in World War III. (That is if there will ever be a world war three."
P is for Popular as I should say "Unicorns are NOT popular!"
E is for Eating. "If unicorns were like cookies, they'd be the next creatures I'd be eating."
R is for Rule. "Horses rule, unicorns drool!"
J is for jeep. "I'd run over Juniper Jade with a super powered jeep."
A is for Apple. "Wouldn't unicorns look better if they were shaped like
    apples?"
D is for Dummy Dufus Dork. That describes unicorns all over.

E is for Enormous. "Juniper gained so much weight, she was nicknamed Enormous!"

I crumpled up the paper and threw it away. "Maybe I just haven't been getting enough sleep lately. If I continue like this, I'll go crazy," I thought.

My feelings were later lifted at suppertime when Sophie stopped by for a visit. She tried her very best to cheer me up. I tried to be happy, but in the end, I felt all gloomy. "Did you want to see my new published article," she finally asked. "Sure. Anything that will help me forget about the circus," I said flatly. Sophie told me that she left the magazine on our coffee table which was in the living room. But when we first set foot in the living room, I glanced at the table and saw that it was GONE! "Oh no! Where could it be?" she cried. "Somebody must have taken it!" I gasped. Just then, we heard a toilet flush and Royal Romeo came skipping out of the nearest bathroom.

"Have you seen Sophie's magazine?" I asked worriedly. "Why should I care? Ask that question yourself!" he snapped. "Hmm," thought Sophie as she walked into the bathroom and surprisingly saw that her magazine was on the floor! "Whew!" she sighed with relief and continued, "Now let me show you that article. You're gonna like it, Susae. The magazine editor sent me an email telling how much she liked the way I wrote and . . . wait a minute, I was sure it was on this page . . . or maybe the next . . . it was on page forty two . . . but where is it?" Sophie frantically flipped through the pages with shaking hands.

"It looks like page forty two isn't there! I see forty one, but it skips straight to forty four! I don't understand!" "Why don't we look in the table of contents?" I suggested. We turned to the front of the magazine and sure enough, the article was supposed to be on page number FORTY TWO. "Maybe they forgot to put my article in the magazine!" cried Sophie. "You said it was in there earlier, Sophie. Maybe it was on another page," I said hopefully. "I checked the whole magazine and I didn't see it," she whimpered.

"Sophie, how did your magazine end up in the bathroom in the first place?"

"I don't know. I just found it laying on the floor after Royal Romeo appeared."

"Do you think HE took the page?"

"Maybe."

"Let's look at the part of the magazine where your article was supposed to be. We may find some clues."

We took a look and it seemed like someone tore the page out!

"Susae, let's start looking. It has to be around here somewhere!''

We searched the bathtub, and around the sink, but we found nothing leading to our missing page.

"There's only ONE place we haven't looked," I concluded as I headed toward the TOILET.

"No way, Syleria. I don't even want to know if it's in THERE!"

"Well, there's only ONE way to find out."

I lifted up the toilet lid and saw bits and pieces of magazine PAPER floating in the water of the toilet bowl!

"Uh, Sophie. I hate to say this, but I think your article has gone bye bye."

"NOOOO!!!!!!!" screamed Sophie as she looked down to see what I saw.

EVERYONE rushed to the bathroom to find Sophie sobbing and me trying to find out how all this had happened. Mrs. Louis tried to comfort Sophie and reassure her that Royal Romeo would be sent to the store immediately to purchase another copy of the magazine. Even the rest of the club members seemed to feel sorry for Sophie's sudden loss.

Part IX: Vanessa Pana

It was August 12th, the day I would go to the circus with Sophie and Patience. Yesterday, Mrs. Louis forced Royal Romeo to replace Sophie's magazine. I could tell that he was NOT happy. For some reason, I felt sorry for Sophie. She had come all the way to OUR house to cheer up Syleria, and instead it turned out that Sophie became gloomy too. Does our household have a contagious disease of the "Gloomy Blues?" If

so, how come I feel so excited? If
it's not only Susae who's sad,
it's Delilah Mara complaining
about her bug bites and unusual
body transformation, Royal Romeo
listening to his favorite music on
his mp3 player to get rid of the
thoughts of unicorns, Mr. Louis
complaining about the unpaid
bills, or Mrs. Louis's attitude
changing to a new dimension with
the income of more housework.

Maybe I shouldn't discuss all
the negative stuff, since now I'm
starting to catch a case of the
Gloomy Blues too. I woke up at
seven in the morning and my
friends picked me up at eight. It
took us two hours to reach the Los
Angeles Circus, which would
actually take place in a REAL
circus tent! What surprised me was
that Juniper Jade looked kind of
different? She was dressed up in a
ballerina outfit and tap dance
shoes. But that wasn't all. She
also performed the exact same
tricks she had done at the zoo. Oh
well, it was fun seeing her
perform. You could watch that
unicorn and never get tired of
watching what she does.

At the end of her performance, her grand finale was also different. The ring master grabbed our attention and announced, "We have a special act to perform, but we need your help." The ring master explained that the unicorn could answer almost any "yes" or "no" questions. So practically the whole audience stood in a long, long, line with questions for the unicorn to answer. As each person took their turn, Sophie scribbled down more notes on her notepad for her next article. The magazine company was extremely impressed with her last article and now she's a member of the Junior Kids Magazine with a job of writing articles.

Usually people who try to get a place in the magazine company only to do one article and are fired. Preteen reporters usually don't get this far in the magazine business, but as long as Sophie's articles are in tip top shape, who knows where this job will take her? Back to the subject. People asked questions like:

"Was my birthday yesterday?"
"Yes."

"Is blue cotton candy better than pink cotton candy?"   "No."

"Was Coca Cola one of the first soft drinks invented?"   "Yes."

The unicorn would nod or shake her head with no hesitation. "Wow! She's pretty smart!" exclaimed Sophie's Dad who couldn't believe what he had seen. Sure enough, Juniper Jade had ALL the correct answers for ALL questions. The first question was asked by a six year old boy who had forgotten if his birthday had passed or not. The unicorn nodded its head and the boy's mother was impressed.

According to a survey taken a few years ago by kids ages five to eighteen, pink cotton candy was better than blue. Juniper Jade had never even seen or heard about the survey! The third question she knew because Juniper drinks Coca Cola sometimes and once she researched in an encyclopedia about the drink. Imagine a unicorn reading! What a day! It looks like I have A LOT to tell Susae!

I hope she won't seem too disappointed. Just in case, I had taken several photo shoots of the unicorn. Ok, maybe not several, but A LOT. Even though nobody will believe in the Juniper, I know I will. I don't get why everyone thinks Juniper is such a big fake! By her beauty and intelligence, she's a WONDER! Hey, isn't that the title that Sophie wanted to choose for her next article? I think it's called:

THE WONDER UNICORN

Or something like that, but still, I can't wait to see what happens as we still continue our mission to solve our mystery of Juniper Jade. Keep reading to find out what happened as we have many decisions to face! Hopefully this book will keep you busy!

Chapter 7: The State Parade Announcement

It was August 13th, Sunday, the day after the circus trip. It was lunchtime and our meal was nothing new. Mrs. Louis fixed us some spinach sandwiches and leaf crackers, one of her new concoctions made from leaves, strips of bark, seasoning herbs, weed stems, and healthy tasting flower petals. As always, Delilah Mara's body turned green with brown stripes and her fur was pink, red, yellow, and purple like the flower petals.

Yesterday, Mrs. Louis had taken Delilah to the vet and surprisingly, her disease seemed unpredictable, meaning that not even the smartest veterinarians at the vet clinic knew what was wrong with Delilah. "WHAT?!? That's preposterous! It has to be something!" Mrs. Louis yelled impatiently. Her lovely brown hair puffed up and her eyes turned an angry red. Startled by her reaction, the vet said, "It's probably just an allergic skin reaction or virus of some sort. We do have some canine doggy pills to soothe the infections, but I'm afraid we can't completely cure the disease without knowing what it really is."

The vet disappeared from the room and came back with a small tray with tweezers, cotton swabs, and other materials. I knew at once what he was going to do. Delilah's eyeballs widened as she saw the vet pick up a needle. Delilah was in for an injection and right away she fainted on the examination table. "Well, at least that makes it easy. At least, she won't feel much of the pain," the vet reassured. The shot lasted only a few seconds and the vet promised to make a call as soon as there were any signs or results.

Mrs. Louis carried Delilah back to where our car was parked and headed for home. There just seemed to be no cure for this unexpected illness. Ok, back to lunchtime.

Mrs. Louis thought we looked so gloomy that she turned on the radio so we could hear some nice and quiet classical music like the "Fantasy Ballad" and "Unicorns on

Ice Symphony." After a few songs ended, we heard a radio announcer tell some more news on Juniper Jade. She would be the main theme attraction of an upcoming California State Parade! This parade comes once a year, but this year the unicorn would be in it. I expected applause and cheering from my friends, but I didn't expect a negative outcome.

"That sounds nice," said Mrs. Louis quietly. For some reason, it looked like she hadn't paid much attention. "Boy was that trashy!" groaned Gabriel with a frown. Allie Angie didn't say much but, "I'm not hungry" and she walked out of the dining room. "Everyone's gonna be sorry once they figure out that Juniper is nothing but a party dressed clown with a glued on horn," declared Delilah. "Yeah, I don't even feel sorry for those people in our country who are wasting their money to buy those useless tickets," added Pierre.

For the next few minutes, everyone was quiet until Delilah spoke up, "Can we change the radio station? I'm getting bored." For some expected reason, I felt like surfing through the internet. I wanted to know LOTS MORE about the unicorn. I think Sophie's article might need a little more information. This could be a chance to find more. But I'll tell you what kind of unexpected thing happened.

While I was scanning through a list of links, a website called, "Juniper Jade the Fake!" caught my eye! I clicked and a page of words appeared. Maybe I shouldn't have read through the article, but my curiosity just got me. As I read, I felt my eyes getting wet. The article was about nothing, but criticism. It stated that after Juniper Jade was shown at a zoo event, news reporters have seen weird things about her.

Before the zoo closed, Juniper was posing for some photo shoots. But suddenly, it started to rain. At first, it sprinkled, but the rain came pouring on everyone AND Juniper Jade! A cameraman claims that he saw the unicorn's horn wobble and the article also showed a short clip of what had happened. Juniper's mane and tail lost their fresh strawberry color and turned a dull gray. The same thing happened to Juniper's body, eyes, and horn. They all lost their color and the unicorn no longer looked like a wonder.

People who were watching all this started to shout words of criticism. But worst of all, they threw popcorn, food, beer, and weeds at Juniper and Matthew Snicket, her trainer. It was a horrible sight and it took quite some time before some police guards settled the angry riot. I couldn't believe what I had seen. And all along Delilah Mara was right. We had wasted our time on something that was fake, not real; you get the picture. I didn't want to believe what I had seen. I didn't want to admit that I saw the truth, but I knew that it had to be done.

Chapter 8: The Unicorn "LIVE" at the Parade

Syleria Susae must have heard me sniffling because she asked, "What's wrong?" I pointed to the computer screen and left the room. Later on, I sat on the couch. I was done crying and the only thing I did was stare at the sweatshirt I bought at the zoo. For some reason, it had no value in my life. Have you ever felt like you did something that wasn't worth it? That's how I felt. Ever since the beginning of the month, I believed in a fake. How unintelligent was that? Syleria Susae came and sat down beside me. "So I guess this is it," she said quietly. I nodded with a blank expression. Mrs. Louis walked in a few minutes later. "What's wrong?" she asked worriedly. "Look at the computer screen," muttered Syleria.

After several minutes, Mrs. Louis came back with two handkerchiefs. She seemed disappointed too. Not only did Mrs. Louis give me and Syleria a hug, but she invited the rest of the club as well. What surprised me was that my friends didn't seem the least bit sad! "So now you know that unicorns are NOT real!" declared Delilah. "Mara, stop it! How would you feel if you were in the same situation? Syleria and Vanessa believed in Juniper Jade all this time and now they suddenly find out that Jade is just a regular horse. You should show respect to others no matter what they may encounter. EVERYONE has a right to believe in ANYTHING!" stated Mrs. Louis. Now that shut Delilah up. Mrs. Louis continued, "Even though Juniper Jade may be just a regular horse, that doesn't mean you still can't go to the parade to see her performances. I can take you if you want."

Syleria Susae and I looked up and slowly nodded our heads. The thought of seeing Juniper Jade again brought a strange feeling over me. Imagine all the children across the country who will come and see Juniper, not knowing that she was just a regular horse with a painted body, confetti hair, and a glued on horn. It was too disappointing to be true. I felt cheated! I had really wasted all these days on a fake! "What a foolish dog I am," I thought.

It was Tuesday, August 15th, the day of the state parade. The parade would take place in Sacramento. I woke up at five in the morning and at six, we took a long car trip to the parade. At noon, we gathered around streets in the city of Sacramento. If you didn't know, Mr. Louis had taken a day off of work so he could take care of my friends while Mrs. Louis took Syleria and I to the parade.

At first, there were only a couple of adults, but in minutes there were crowds of hundreds and hundreds of children with their parents. They all wanted to see the unicorn. This all just seemed totally WRONG! A marching band came through the street playing some music and the unicorn was in the lead dressed in a hat and cape that was colored red, white, and blue. I felt a tap on my shoulder and I saw Patience and Sophie with Mrs. LeLaine! "Mrs. Louis emailed us about the unicorn and we came to cheer you up!" said Patience.

"Really?" I asked hopefully. "Of course! What are friends for, anyway? I also have to write my next article so it's about time I take notes," Sophie added showing us her notepad. Right after Sophie had finished talking, a gust of wind blew in our faces and dark, black clouds formed in the sky.

The crowd of people looked up in dismay and the band stopped playing as an instant shower of pouring rain splashed over the city! Little children cried and parents screamed as nearby store windows shattered and traffic lights fell to the street in pieces! But worst of all, was Juniper Jade! Most of her fur had fallen out and in seconds she was almost BALD! That wasn't all; Jade's eyes, horn, and body turned a dark brown and her horn sway from side to side! "Oh no! It looks like her horn might fall off!" cried Mrs. LeLaine. Groups of people shouted at Matthew Snicket, criticizing, throwing things, and wanting refunds! News reporters and cameramen snapped photos and managed to catch everything on tape for the WHOLE country to see!

I couldn't stand to see any more and Mrs. Louis immediately took us home. Supper was quite awkward. Most of the club members seemed quite happy, including Delilah Mara! I trudged to my room after I chugged down some more vegetables. "I hate all this!" I thought. Just like that wasn't enough to make me gloomy, I spotted a piece of paper on my dresser drawer. It obviously turned out to be from Delilah Mara. It read:

Beware of Juniper Jade the Horrendous, Hideous, Ghastly, Evil, Ugly, Powerless Monster!!!!

Chapter 9: The View

It was Friday, August 18th and everything seemed the same as it was before when I never knew about the unicorn. Nobody except Syleria Susae mentioned anything about Juniper Jade. It seemed like Mrs. Louis could no longer stand my misery. "I have A LOT of things on my shopping list and I could sure have someone run by the store to buy them," she suggested. So it was settled. Syleria Susae and I would take a small trip to the grocery store to buy eggs, milk, and cereal. What surprised was that as soon as we entered the store, everything seemed NORMAL! What I mean by normal was that ALL the products in the store except the Clearance Section had not a single unicorn on them.

The eggs were pure white, the milk cartons had no unicorn labels, and there were no unicorns in or on our cereal! We bought our items and arrived home. Sadly, Mrs. Louis's cheerful expression faded. "It looks like the stores are no longer selling unicorn merchandise," she sighed. "Well,

I'm happy with that," cheered Delilah Mara as she happily came into the kitchen. "So am I!" squealed Allie Angie. "Forget about the outhouse idea! Now I can use a regular bathroom again!" agreed Pierre.

I was just about to go to my room when I instantly heard the phone ring. I picked it up and it turned out to be from Sophie LeLaine!

Sophie – "Vanessa, you can't believe this, but I have some good news!"

Vanessa – "What?"

S – "It looks like the unicorn, I mean, Juniper Jade has been sent to a nearby farm which is one mile away from my neighborhood!"

V – "No way!"

S –"Yes way! Matthew Snicket phoned me and told me so. Do you want to come over to my house? My mom can drive you, Susae, Patience, and I over to the farm."

V – "Ok!"

I hung up and asked Mrs. Louis for permission and then I told the news to Syleria. "I don't know. I mean, the unicorn isn't real and I've been making a total fool of myself by believing that it was," she said sadly. "Please? Just one last time?" I pleaded. "Oh, all right. But you know that I'm still NOT gonna be happy," she groaned.

In minutes we arrived at Sophie's house and in another ten minutes, we found ourselves in front of a bright red barn near fields and hills of farmland. Sophie's mom went to a house nearby to talk to the farmer who was looking after Juniper Jade. It was still daylight outside and in half an hour, it would be six o' clock.

The barn looked like an ordinary barn. It was red with white stripes and fields that fenced in animals and crops were around it. Sophie opened the heavy barn door and inside were stalls and mounds of hay. It smelled like dirty animals in here! A small herd of chickens came to greet us and pigs, sheep, cattle and horses glanced our way. We ventured through the whole barn and in a dark corner was a small stall where Juniper Jade stood with her head down and a gloomy expression. Surprisingly, her mane and tail had grown back and it seemed like she regained her magic unicorn colors again.

We each said goodbye to the unicorn or should I say, the horse. Sophie was just about the touch Juniper's horn, when Patience stated, "It's no use, Sophie. We already know she's just a regular horse." At that remark, Juniper whinnied sadly and turned her head to look out a nearby window. "You have to admit it, Juniper. You may be able to do great things, but you're just a regular horse," said Syleria. "I'm getting hungry. Do you think the farmer has any food around here?" I asked. "Good question. I'm getting hungry too," Patience added.

So we took one last look at the unicorn and closed the big, wooden, heavy barn doors. When we walked inside the farmer's house, we saw Sophie's mom and the farmer seated at a table in a dining room with cups of coffee with some desert. "We're hungry and we were wondering if there was anything to eat," Sophie explained. "It's a good thing you stopped by. If you didn't know, I'm Matthew Snicket's brother. I have some delicious homemade cinnamon rolls and milk. Care to join me?" answered the farmer. "Sure!" Sophie replied.

We took our seats at the table. Here's some more info for you to know: The farmer had a pretty small house and I wouldn't say it was very fancy. It had a bathroom, a dining room, a bedroom, a kitchen, and a living room just like any other small house would. Except the walls were covered in orange wall paper and paintings of farms and animals were posted on the wall. Even dishes were decorated with animals and the pantry was filled with "farm" food. And what I mean by farm food was that the pantry was filled with food that came from the farm like eggs from chickens, milk from cattle, bacon from pigs, chicken legs from chickens, and vegetables with crops.

Syleria Susae was busily listening to the conversation that Mrs. LeLaine and Mr. Snicket were having. Patience was busily chugging down one cinnamon roll after another. Sophie was taking more notes on the last unicorn article she would be writing. And me? Well, I just sat and listened to what was going on. This is sort of how everything sounded like:

Mrs. LeLaine – "Do you like it out here in the open country?'
Patience – munch, crunch, GULP!!!
Syleria – "Hmm."
Sophie – scribble, scribble, scribble
Mr. Snicket – "Oh yes! As a matter of fact, I raise LOTS of animals, including this new litter of piglets that were recently born."
Patience – munch, crunch, COUGH!!!
Sophie – scribble, scratch, erase, scribble
Mrs. LeLaine – "I bet you don't have to go to the store to buy breakfast."
Syleria – Yawn.
Patience – cough, hiccup, hiccup, HICCUP!!!

Mr. Snicket – "Oh no, not at all. Whenever I want scrambled eggs and bacon, I just fetch a pig and a couple of eggs. I know the chickens don't really appreciate it, but I have to eat sometime soon or later and it sure saves A LOT of money."

Sophie - scribble, flip, scribble
Syleria - sigh.
Patience - GULP, munch, ACHOO!!!

This all went on and on for only a few minutes, but to me it seemed like hours and hours. All windows of the farmer's house were open and I could hear the crows cawing, pigs oinking, cattle mooing, and chickens clucking. I couldn't stand all this noise! I wonder how the farmer can deal with this. If it was up to me, I'd tie duck tape around all these animals' mouths to get some peace and quiet.

I just sat there listening to all this confusion when I heard a sudden CRASH!!! And then a BANG!!! And lastly, a heavy THUD!!! Everyone automatically shouted, "WHAT WAS THAT?!?"

In seconds, we rushed to the barn to see that the barn doors were knocked off their hinges and were laying flat on the ground in pieces. Mr. Snicket quickly ran inside the barn saying, "You guys stay outside and I'll see what's going on!" Sophie's mom kept us all back and the sight of destruction and farm animals wondering around the place made me wonder and think about what had just happened. How did all this occur? What caused the noise? Is Juniper okay? Mr. Snicket came zooming out of the barn dismayed with tears in his eyes crying, "Juniper Jade is GONE! We need to find her! I promised my brother and Robert Portman that'd take extra special care of her!"

Mrs. LeLaine gasped and we started searching. The wind outside was blowing quite hard and I caught some dust in my eyes. As I looked up to the skies, I saw a horse shaped figure flying away! This seemed too unbelievable to be true!

Chapter 10: Juniper Jade & Her Magic World

Today was Monday, August 21st. I bet you're wondering what happened yesterday. The only ones who knew about the little horse shaped flying figure in the sky was Sophie and me. Mrs. LeLaine, Sophie, Patience, Syleria and I helped Mr. Snicket search for Juniper Jade even though Sophie and I were aware of what we had seen. Sophie had also looked in the sky and had seen the figure. "Was that really Juniper FLYING in the sky? It could have just been a small airplane. But then again, how many airplanes in this world are shaped like horses?" I thought.

We search the whole farm and after an hour, we were about ready to give up. It was getting late and Mrs. LeLaine had to take us home. If you thought that day was quite disappointing, our luck actually turned up a little later. It was five o' clock and Sophie and I decided to play ball in the park that was a couple of blocks away from my apartment. Patience was busy with chores and Syleria had gone clothes shopping with Mrs. Louis. In a few days Sophie would start school and we wanted to spend some time together before that would happen.

The park we were playing in was called Nature View. Nature View really did have a view! It was really an extremely tall hill where there were lots of trees. You can practically see the WHOLE county! Well, some of it, anyway. In the very center of the hill was a clearing with lots of flowers, a playground, a small lake, and best of all, a large space to fly kites, set up a picnic, OR play ball!

Sophie and I were playing soccer! I passed the ball to Sophie and she kicked it so high that it flew into the sky, out of our sight, and into some trees. We searched behind almost every tree, but there was still no sign of our missing soccer ball! "I paid TWENTY dollars for that ball!" cried Sophie. "Don't worry, we'll find it," I reassured as I began to look behind a pine tree. "Hopefully it should be somewhere around here . . . WHOA!!!" Sophie turned around asking, "What is it? Is something wrong?" She gasped as she saw that before her eyes was Juniper Jade! Beside her was OUR soccer ball! The unicorn began to SPEAK, "Greetings, friends. I found this round object and I wondered if it might be yours." "Uh, uh, why yes, it certainly is!" Sophie stammered as she quickly snatched her ball. "What are YOU doing here?" I asked suspiciously. "I am Juniper Jade, the magic unicorn. I am running away from Earth and rejoining my own kind of planet Sao Myrad Suath. I decided to stop by and eat some grass before I continued on my way. I find Earth's grass not so appetizing, though, but it's better than nothing," Juniper continued.

"You may talk and you may perform some of the greatest tricks ever known, but you'll never convince me to believe you are a true unicorn," Sophie snapped. "Try taking off my horn. Then you will see if I am real or not," Juniper commanded. Sophie reached out slowly to touch the horn. With her hand, she took a tough grip and pulled. She checked all edges of the base of the horn. In a few seconds, she gasped saying, "It won't come off! I don't even see any tape or glue!"

"Juniper, I have one question. If you're a real unicorn, why do you lose your fur and color sometimes? I thought unicorns had special powers. I just don't get it," I said. Juniper sighed and explained, "We unicorns come from an unknown world. Sometimes our powers cannot stand Earth's weather." "Oh," said Sophie. Now all this seemed to make sense! "I would like you grant you each a wish," Juniper offered. "I wish my friend Delilah Mara would get cured from her bug bite disease," I requested. "I wish for the intelligence to be smart when school starts again," Sophie added. Immediately, magic sparkles came out of Juniper's horn and we knew at once that our wishes had been granted! "I feel smarter!" Sophie exclaimed. "But before I go, I'll show you a tour of my magic home, the planet of Sao Myrad Suath. You must climb on my back. This should not take much time at all," said Juniper Jade.

We hopped upon Juniper's back
and in seconds, we were high up
above the park and above our town.
Below were lights of buildings,
people, and cars. Higher and
higher we went above the sky.
After five minutes, we passed
through our atmosphere. The wind
was blowing in our faces, but
Juniper didn't seem to mind.
Sophie looked up and gasped, "We
won't be able to make it! We'll
die without oxygen!" I looked
toward the direction we were
heading and outer space was only
about one or two miles ahead!
Sophie was right! What could we
do? Then all of a sudden, a bubble
formed around us and we could
breathe easily. "I think this is
an oxygen bubble," I thought. The
next thing I knew, we were in
outer space!

By high speed, we passed by
each planet constantly having to
avoid crashing into moons,
meteors, asteroids, or even the
planets themselves. I wish I would
have brought a camera. Then I
could take photos of the planets
and I would be famous! After we
finally passed Pluto, the only
thing we saw ahead at that point

were stars. When approximately twenty minutes had passed, I noticed that the stars were rainbow colored and shaped like unicorns! According to Juniper, we had entered ANOHER galaxy! I knew right at once that we were close to Juniper's home planet! In a far distance was a planet of gold, sliver, bronze, and sapphire colors. About seven rings encircled the planet. It looked sort of like Saturn, except three rings were around the planet and four rings circled the from the bottom to the top of the planet. We saw several unicorns flying from the planet to meet Juniper!

Each unicorn was of different colors! My guess was that this was Juniper's FAMILY! I saw two older unicorns and a few smaller ones. Yep! It looked like a family of unicorns! "I shall return home and so shall you. You have been great companions. I hope we see each other soon," said Juniper sadly. We gave Juniper a BIG hug and asked, "But how do we get home? We can't fly!"

Juniper pointed her horn at a magic whirlpool beside us

explaining, "Jump off of my back
and into the whirlpool. It should
take you home." The whirlpool was
right beside us and it was pink
with white swirling stars. With
our greatest effort, we leaped and
in the blink of an eye, we were
back on the top of Nature View.
Juniper was gone and so was the
planet and outer space. We had
returned to Earth in no time at
all! Sophie glanced at her watch
and warned, "We'd better get home!
It's almost seven o' clock!" I
looked around and sure enough, the
sun was setting and the moon was
in view. Sophie and I climbed down
the hill and walked a couple of
blocks past houses, stores, and
other places to our homes. I felt
like what had just happened was
just a dream, but when I thought
about the planets I had seen, I
quickly knew that what I had seen
and experienced was REAL! Now I
will say that this was the end of
our adventure.

THE END!!!

EPILOGUE: THE CONCLUSION

Wait a minute! Don't leave just yet! I bet you're still wondering what happened after Juniper returned home. Well here it goes. I just couldn't believe I had traveled in space, out of this universe, to another galaxy! Now you can finally ask that question of yours. Is Juniper Jade a real unicorn? Well, now you know the answer to that question which is YES! Imagine how we went through all these days dealing over the debate of a unicorn. So much has been done and seen.

When I got home, I was able to tell Syleria Susae EVERYTHING I saw! But surprisingly, she started CRYING! Not crying sadness, but tears of joy and happiness and accomplishment and grace and love and every happy thing you could EVER think of. We found out if Juniper Jade was real which meant we had solved ANOTHER mystery! The Dream Detectives Dog Club had now achieved their own goals. This has been our second mystery and it has been a great success! We helped our county find stolen items from a museum in our last adventure and now we found out the truth of something that resembled a legend: Juniper Jade!

The good thing was that she was able to get back home to her planet, her environment, her family, her friends, and to the place she really belongs. I'm glad no one has sent satellites past Pluto or else Juniper's unknown world might not become so unknown. I hope her planet stays secret for as long as she lives. If our country found out unicorns existed, the world would go wild! That's not all! Plus, Delilah Mara was back to normal with not a single bug bite!

You should have seen the look on everyone's faces. Mrs. Louis totally freaked out and called the vet right away saying, "The bug bites have finally gone away!" The vet replied, "It must have been all the medicine she took! What a miracle!"

Everyone except Sophie, Patience, Syleria and I knew what REALLY cured Delilah. Not only is that all I have to say, but here's what I have been waiting and waiting to tell you ever since you started reading our tale: The moral of this mystery is "Seeing is more than just Believing." You have to take risks and chances to prove your opinion. Take Syleria and I for an example. We were so determined to find out for ourselves what the REAL answer was instead of jumping to conclusions like everyone else did. We have many more adventures to tell you, but for now I'm taking a break! Hope to see ya around!

Bye for now, Vanessa Pana your canine friend!

OFFICIALLY THE END!!!
(Or is it just the beginning of ??? . . . .)

Final Words from the Author

Dear Reader
You have read one of my first few published books and in this fun tale, you learned how sometimes you have to prove your own opinions. Susae and Pana were great examples as they teamed together to search for an answer to their mind echoing question. I encourage other to be influenced by these two characters. I always used to like unicorns when I was younger and at times, I really wished they were real. So I wrote this book to open up the imagination of me and others as we explore the wonders of a known myth, the unicorn. I dedicate this book to those who have read it and are willing to read more adventures that will be coming in this new series! With the help of my inspiration and my friends of the Dream Detectives Dog Club (which is fiction, by the way), we can truly influence others and make our world a better place! We expand our wonders and thoughts and take a journey to see if it comes true! If I wouldn't have

been influenced by my life and those who have helped me, this series and its characters would not have been born!

See ya later, Sarah Cantu aka Kitty!

About the Author

Sarah Veronica Cantu also nicknamed Kitty Can 2 is twelve years old and was born in McAllen, Texas. She is currently attending Kingsway Christian School. Her origins are Hispanic, Mexican Indian, Italian, a little bit of Irish and Asian, and possibly Middle Eastern and African. Her natural hair color is black, but it's now dyed dark red and her eyes are dark brown. She is the oldest daughter of Ricardo and Veronica Cantu and she has two little brothers and one little sister, Jacob (1999), Hannah (2001), and Richard (2006). She has been publishing since 2005 and her hobbies are art, story writing, singing, and composing music. Her favorite sports are volleyball, basketball, and hockey!

Personal Interview:
Hey! It's me, the young author! I've accomplished MANY things this year and I thank all my friends who have supported me in EVERY way. School is gonna be ending and that gives me time to think of more adventures to add to my new series! Syleria and Vanessa really enjoy hearing from their fans and so do I. Hopefully, I'll be gathering some more inspiration for the Dream Detectives Dog Club, who are eagerly looking forward to another adventure! Are you? If so, keep reading! There's more to hear

and later on this year, you'll hear of more mysteries to solve!
Other Info:
Favorite Singers; Sheryl Crow, Ashlee Simpson, Avril Lavigne, Jump 5
Favorite colors: gold, silver, red, purple, white, black, light blue
Favorite Actors: Dakota Fanning, Angelina Jolie, Sarah Michelle Gellar
Favorite animal: CATS!!! I like Siamese, Maine Coons, and Turkish Vans
Favorite Instruments: piano, percussion, guitar, and saxophones!
Favorite amusement park: Kings Island!!!

Suggested Further Reading

<u>Coming Soon: The adventures
continue!!!</u>

The Dogs that Follow their
Detective Dreams # 4: The Secret
of the New Cat.

<u>Similar Books:</u>

The Dogs that Follow their
Detective Dreams # 2: The Mystery
of the Stolen Gemstones.

The Feline & K9 Companions (a
new series!)

Feline & K9 Companions # 1:
The Mystery of the Stolen
Valuables!